She smiled at him. It was a pathetic excuse for a smile, she could tell, but he looked so worried about her. "I know. It's not my fault."

"Do you know?" Scott leaned closer. "Because it sure seems like you've been carrying this around with you for a year."

She had. The guilt was always there. And now that Connors was out of jail, asking for her help, there was no way to hide from it anymore. If she could start working through the consequences of that day, maybe it was time to stop hiding from what had happened with Scott, too.

Maybe it was time to stop denying that she had genuine feelings for this man. Figuring out what exactly those feelings were was the hard part. But the thought of him with someone else filled her with jealousy. And the way he was staring at her now, with so much concern and caring, made need rise up inside her. A need to feel his arms around her again, to feel his lips on hers.

To be with him just one more time.

Seduced
by the Sniper

ELIZABETH
HEITER

First published in Great Britain 2015
by Mills & Boon, an imprint of Harlequin (UK) Limited.
Large Print edition 2015
Eton House, 18-24 Paradise Road,
Richmond, Surrey, TW9 1SR

© 2015 by Elizabeth Heiter

ISBN: 978-0-263-26014-4

Harlequin (UK) Limited's policy is to use papers that are natural, renewable and recyclable products and made from wood grown in sustainable forests. The logging and manufacturing processes conform to the legal environmental regulations of the country of origin.

Printed and bound in Great Britain
by CPI Antony Rowe, Chippenham, Wiltshire

ELIZABETH HEITER

likes her suspense to feature strong heroines, chilling villains, psychological twists and a little romance. Her research has taken her into the minds of serial killers, through murder investigations and onto the FBI Academy's shooting range. Elizabeth graduated from the University of Michigan with a degree in English literature. She's a member of International Thriller Writers and Romance Writers of America. Visit Elizabeth at elizabethheiter.com

For Kristen Kobet. Since the day
we became dorm-mates back in college,
you've been my third sister.

Chapter One

June, one year ago

Scott Delacorte was a lucky man.

Meeting women had always come easily for him. He'd long ago perfected the subtle charm that drew women in, and the easygoing, never serious attitude that kept them from staying too long. His only rules were no married women and no fellow FBI agents.

Last night, he'd broken the second rule.

Scott rolled over in bed, his eyes closed, still blissed out from a night with newly minted negotiator Chelsie Russell. Tall, blonde and blue-eyed, she looked more like a cover model than an FBI agent, but the thing that had sucked Scott in was her smile. Too big for her face and way too infectious, it came with an impressive ability to read people and a willingness to go toe-to-toe with any agent at Shields Tavern. Including him. And he'd been more than eager to take her up on the challenge.

He'd met her before, in passing. She'd joined the FBI a year after him, with his sister Maggie and their close friend Ella, and over the years, he'd seen her with them. But he'd never really talked to her until last night.

She'd shown up at Shields as he was walking to the door. He'd just said goodbye to his fellow agents from the Hostage Rescue Team when she'd walked in, already grinning. And he'd turned right back around, pushed by a few other guys who'd noticed her, too, and introduced himself. He bought her a drink when she told him she was celebrating officially becoming an FBI negotiator.

He'd done his best to monopolize her at the

bar, but he'd been sure she'd turn him down when he invited her back to his place. Instead, she set down her drink, threaded her fingers through his and suggested he lead the way.

In bed, eyes still closed, Scott breathed in the scent of her strawberry shampoo and reached for her. He'd finally fallen asleep sometime after 4:00 a.m., and his internal clock told him it couldn't be much past seven now. But he was already craving the feel of her long hair draped around his face, her nails skimming over his back as she kissed him. His fingers stretched across the bed, searching, but all he felt was empty sheets, still warm on her side.

Opening his eyes, Scott glanced around his bedroom. Empty.

He sat up, stifling a yawn, and peered toward the bathroom. The door was open. She wasn't in there. Last night, he'd strewn both of their clothes all over the room. Now hers were missing.

Cursing, he jumped out of bed. He still felt her

warmth on his sheets, so she couldn't have been up long. Not bothering to get dressed, he hurried through his small bungalow to the entryway.

He lived in rural Virginia, so he didn't have to worry about curious neighbors as he opened the door and peered outside.

Her car was gone.

Scott stared at the empty drive for a minute before slowly closing the door. She'd actually sneaked out on him. He couldn't believe he hadn't heard her get up. Normally, the smallest noise woke him. But she'd completely worn him out last night. Then slipped away without a word.

He'd had his share of flings, even a few one-night stands, but he'd never sneaked out on anyone. And although he would've bet good money that Chelsie Russell had never had a single fling before last night, he was shocked that she'd slunk off.

It probably served him right. All the years of

never wanting a serious relationship, and the one woman who'd completely captivated him didn't want anything real with *him*.

Still, the knowledge stung. It didn't matter how stupid it might be to expect something real to develop out of a one-night stand. The fact was, he'd already been planning their first real date, and the one after that, before he'd invited her home.

But he hadn't made it into the FBI's elite Hostage Rescue Team by giving up at the first sign of failure. Chelsie's first day as a negotiator at the Washington Field Office started today. The WFO was less than twenty-five miles from Quantico, where HRT was based, and his sister Maggie worked there. It'd be simple to find a way to run into Chelsie. Whatever her reasons for skipping out on him—probably pure and simple embarrassment over jumping in so fast—he planned to use every ounce of charm he had to get her back into his bed, and his life.

He flicked on the coffeepot as he turned back

to his bedroom and was pulling on his pants when his cell phone beeped, loud and insistent.

Scott grabbed it off his nightstand. Triple-eight code. An emergency callout.

His pulse spiked as he yanked on the rest of his clothes, then reached for the gear he'd dumped on his nightstand last night when Chelsie had dragged him toward his bed. He strapped on his holster and picked up his BlackBerry. His tactical bag with his sniper rifle was in the back of his SUV, so he double-timed it out the door as he checked the text on his phone for details.

Active shooter. Location: a community center close to his house. The reported targets: military officers in town for a recruitment booth scheduled to open in half an hour.

HRT was going straight to the site and would set up an immediate command post on the outskirts. The community center was close, so Scott knew he'd beat the rest of his team there. Procedure dictated that he move in as close as he could and set up an observation post. Figure out how many shooters there were, and where they were located. His boss would be close behind him with instructions beyond that.

Scott hopped into his Bureau-issued SUV and sped out of his dirt drive, kicking up dust behind him. As he drove, he called the Special Agent in charge of his team, nicknamed Froggy because he'd come from the Navy SEALs before joining the Bureau.

"What's the situation?" he asked Froggy.

"Details are still sketchy. Call came in to 911 eight minutes ago. Reports are there's a long-distance shooter involved, so the locals want us to take it. CNU is sending one of their best."

CNU was the Crisis Negotiation Unit at Quantico. Typically in charge of training negotiators from the FBI's field offices around the country, they also deployed with HRT for major incidents. Right now, a negotiator at CNU was probably closer than one from the Washington Field Office.

The negotiator would focus on trying to talk

the shooter down peacefully. HRT's job was to provide a tactical solution if that wasn't possible.

"You'll be first on site," Froggy said. "We'll be right behind you. According to the eyewitness, there's only one shooter."

He didn't have to tell Scott that what that really meant was they had no idea how many shooters there were. Witness reports were notoriously unreliable.

Barreling down the rural highway toward the site of the shooting, his siren blaring, Scott asked, "How many civilians?"

"Don't know. The community center wasn't open yet, but the call came in from a secretary who works there. She and another worker managed to get out of the building and to their cars. She says she thinks the only ones left at the center are the army officers."

"I don't suppose they're armed?"

"I don't think so."

The answer was partly good—it meant he

wouldn't have to worry about being shot by a friendly. And it was partly bad—the targets couldn't protect themselves. Scott punched down harder on the gas and shut off his siren. "I'm less than a minute out."

"Watch yourself," Froggy said. "I'll be there in five."

Scott had been called to a lot of shootings since he'd joined HRT. Sometimes the shooters were experienced, sometimes they relied on dumb luck and firepower. But the fact that a long-distance shooter was involved meant they were responding with extra caution, especially since he couldn't be sure there was only one of them.

He drove his SUV to a line of trees outside the community center, slamming to a stop underneath them. Beside him was the back parking lot; he knew there was another lot at the front of the building. As he shimmied into his bullet-proof vest and strapped on the extra gear he'd need, the crack of a rifle split the air.

Swearing, Scott stayed low as he went around to the back of his vehicle for his gear, scanning the area as he moved. The shot had come from the front of the center, but that didn't mean a second shooter wasn't out here.

He quickly counted ten cars in the back parking lot, the early June sunlight glinting off the windshields. If one belonged to the shooter, that left at least nine innocents.

The back lot was empty of people, which meant everyone was either in the front lot, where the shooting was happening, or inside the building. He hoped it was the latter, but if that were the case, Scott knew he probably wouldn't be hearing gunshots right now.

Sweat gathered at his temples, but his heart rate stayed steady. This was the job. It never got routine, but HRT practiced with live fire and he'd taken a lot of calls in the past six months. He'd discovered his tendency was to stay calm until it was all over. Then his adrenaline rush would fade and the reality of what had happened would sink in.

Right now, he needed to assess. His gut instinct was that the single shooter theory was right, but he wasn't going to take that as a given until he'd confirmed it with his own eyes.

Scott yanked his Remington rifle, complete with a custom scope, out of his tactical bag. Keeping low, he raced for the corner of the building where he could peek around to the front and evaluate. Being first on scene, he was Sierra One: sniper position one, closest to the action.

It was exactly where he liked to be, although usually he found the high ground and set up with a lot more care, with the time to scout out exactly the right angles for all his teammates. Right now, with an active shooter, every second could cost lives.

Crouching down, Scott grabbed his tactical mirror and stretched it past the edge of the building, scanning.

He held in a curse as he realized the recruitment booth had been set up in the front parking lot. He spotted four men down beside the table, clearly dead, and three others sprawled near the door, likely hit as they'd made a run for the entrance. Two more were lying behind the community-center sign in pools of blood. If the shooter had hit them there, it meant he had high ground, that he'd found a perch with an angle sharp enough to see the men over the top of the sign.

He couldn't be positive until he checked pulses, but he was pretty sure he was too late to help any of them. Scott reined in his anger and helplessness and thought strategically, the way HRT had taught him.

It was likely the tenth car in the lot belonged to the shooter. But where was he? Scott rotated the mirror again, searching, when it was ripped out of his fingers, the sound of a rifle booming.

Scott shook out his hand, which burned from the force of the mirror being shot out of it, and sunk low. He no longer had a visual and no way was he sticking his head around that corner. In the distance, over the ringing in his ears from the rifle shots, he heard the clang of metal.

The bleachers. On the other side of the community center there had once been a high school. It had been torn down years ago and was now mostly overgrown, but kids played baseball in the field occasionally. The bleachers were still there, the perfect spot for a skilled shooter to lie down and wait.

Scott raced back the way he'd come, taking out his FBI BlackBerry. But as he rounded the back of the building, he discovered he didn't need it. The rest of his team had arrived.

Another sniper and six operators, including Froggy. The operators were fast, strapping on gear from their tactical bags, choosing only the most crucial of the sixty-five pounds of equipment they usually carried.

"What's the situation?" Scott's partner, Andre

Diaz, was already scanning the area with his scope, his normally laid-back expression tense.

"We've got nine down in the front parking lot. Shooter was on the bleachers at the park, about two hundred yards from the front parking lot, but I'm pretty sure he took off. Be careful. This guy shot the tactical mirror right out of my hand."

Grim faces swung toward him.

"You get a vehicle?" Andre asked.

When Scott shook his head, Andre ran for the other side of the building for a different vantage point. Scott started to follow when a sedan swung into the lot, sirens screaming.

Glaring at the newcomer—the CNU negotiator had finally arrived—Scott sliced a hand in front of his neck and the siren went silent.

Martin Jennings, who'd been a negotiator for the Bureau for nearly two decades, hopped out of his car. "Where's Russell?"

Scott froze in the process of chasing after

Andre, but it didn't matter, because his partner was already coming back their way.

"What have you got?" Froggy asked.

"Black Taurus. I got a plate," Andre said. "We'll need to call the locals and have roadblocks set up. He's gone."

"Russell?" Scott asked, his attention fully, anxiously on Martin.

"Chelsie Russell," Martin said. "Brand-new negotiator. I called her to have her meet me here and she was already nearby. She should have beaten me."

Scott glanced at the non-Bureau cars in the lot. Ten cars. And the shooter had been parked over by the bleachers, not here. Was the tenth car Chelsie's? He scanned them, and realized the one way at the back was a small, nondescript white compact. Just like the one Chelsie had driven last night.

Sucking in a hard breath, Scott spun for the front lot again. Behind him, he heard Martin calling for ambulances and Froggy calling the locals to get roadblocks set up. He sensed without glancing back that Andre was following him, that his partner knew something was up.

But all he could think of was Chelsie. He'd seen nine bodies. Was there a tenth?

CHELSIE RUSSELL HUNCHED outside the front door of the community center, shielded on either side by the brick walls of the building that jutted forward, forming a protective U around her. The bullhorn she'd been shouting into less than ten minutes ago hung limply at her side. Above her, the sky was a brilliant, mocking blue.

She was too terrified to move.

A minute ago, the shooter had taken another shot, although at what she had no idea. All his targets were dead. All except her.

He'd been shooting from somewhere off to her right. Was he maneuvering around now, trying to get a bead on her?

She stared at the army officers who'd ducked

down behind the community-center sign, thinking they were safe. He'd picked them off, then shot the three who'd run toward her, ignoring her gestures for them to stay where they were. Nausea rolled through her and she forced herself to look away from the men, their arms splayed wide as if they were still entreating her to help.

They'd been alive a minute ago. Alive and afraid, like her. When she'd crept out the door, she'd seen a sudden burst of hope in their eyes. They'd started to run even though she'd frantically gestured for them to stay put. So she'd put that bullhorn to her lips and done exactly what the FBI had trained her to do.

Connect with the perpetrator. Identify what he wanted. Then convince him through communication tactics that he could achieve it another way.

But he'd ignored every attempt she'd made to talk him down. Resisted every single tactic she'd been taught by the Crisis Negotiation Unit.

She'd gotten here in time. She should have

been able to save five of them. But she hadn't made a bit of difference.

Why hadn't she stayed in Scott Delacorte's bed? Instead of dressing silently and tiptoeing through his house out to her car, she could have rolled over and run her hands over his spectacular body until he'd woken up. Until he'd pressed his lips to hers and made her forget everything but the feel of him on top of her.

Instead, she'd slipped out the door, embarrassed and uncertain after waking up next to a man she barely knew. Before she'd turned off his street, she'd gotten the call from Martin, sending her here. She'd felt a surge of nerves mingled with anticipation and a stupid, baseless confidence that she could change the outcome the shooter had planned today.

Right now, more help was on the way, possibly even Scott himself, but she was the only one left to save. Would they arrive before the shooter found her?

Chelsie eased back toward the door of the

community center, erasing her view of the dead soldiers, of the blood painting the concrete red. Ears ringing from the gunshots, she clutched her Glock so tightly her hand ached. She didn't have the range of a rifle, and whoever had been shooting had been deadly accurate.

She opened the door, staying low, and slipped back inside the community center, her heart beating a too-rapid tempo. A haze fell over her thoughts and she couldn't shake it. Six years in the FBI and she'd never seen anything like this.

Six years in the FBI and she'd never failed like this. She'd joined on a fluke, an attempt to find a place she finally fit. And she thought she had. She'd started in the Los Angeles Field Office, thrown into counterterror as a rookie, and discovered she had a knack for understanding people, agents and criminals alike. That knack had helped her to shed the Barbie-doll nickname she'd been given her first day, and to fit in with the mostly male agents. And it had ultimately led her to negotiation.

Becoming a negotiator had made her feel as though everything in her life had finally snapped into place, as though she'd found where she belonged, the place she could make a real difference.

Resolution through dialogue—it was CNU's motto. In the intense, unforgiving two-week training, she'd excelled. In real life, apparently, she didn't.

Martin Jennings had told her to wait for him before she engaged the shooter. He had more than twenty years' experience talking down dangerous subjects; she had training exercises in a classroom. She'd inched as close to the scene as she dared without putting herself in the line of fire, fully intending to wait. But two people had been shot as she stepped out the door, and she'd known she couldn't sit on the sidelines a second longer.

She'd done her best, and she knew it. But her best hadn't been close to good enough.

Worry about it later, Chelsie told herself, her

eyes darting left and right. She stuck close to the wall as she walked through the empty, silent community center. Then the sound of a siren reached her ears. She let out a relieved breath, but it caught less than a minute later as a shadow passed by the glass door on the side of the building. A tall shadow, carrying a rifle.

Flattening herself against the wall, Chelsie set the bullhorn carefully on the floor so she could grip her Glock with both hands. She inched closer, stepping soundlessly in her practical flats. Her senses seemed to shrink, until all she saw was the glass door to the side of the building, until all she heard was her own even, deep breathing. If there was no talking him down, she wasn't letting the shooter get away, wasn't giving him the chance to go after anyone else. Not today or ever again.

Slowly, slowly, she turned the handle and opened the door, inch by inch. She sensed before she saw that he'd heard her, so she ripped the door open the rest of the way. Her Glock came up fast and steady, taking aim at center mass. "FBI! Don't move!"

She instantly processed the Kevlar vest, the extra weapon strapped to the leg, the Remington rifle in his hands, then recognized more before he finished spinning toward her. The dark blond hair. The tall, lanky body. The long, slim fingers gripping the stock of the rifle.

"Scott," she blurted. The fun-loving, quick-to-smile agent she'd been unable to resist last night seemed like someone else entirely in his tactical gear, his expression fierce and determined.

"Chelsie." Relief bloomed in his chocolate-brown eyes, so strong it made her own eyes water.

Another HRT sniper materialized from around the corner, but she couldn't take her eyes off Scott. Heat rushed up her face, but it wasn't from the embarrassment of being caught in the same clothes he'd peeled off her last night, or from seeing him so soon after sneaking out in the darkness. Seeing Scott couldn't distract her from the weariness and splintering anger she suddenly felt.

Nine people had died today. And it didn't matter what the FBI thought of her actions. Her career as a negotiator had ended before it had even begun.

Chapter Two

June, present day

"You missed a spot," Chelsie told Maggie Delacorte as they walked out of the Washington Field Office.

Scott's younger sister looked nothing like him. A few inches shorter than Chelsie, with dark brown hair cut into a stylish, practical bob, and light blue eyes, Maggie shared only one thing with her brother: the intensity in their gaze. Or two, counting their willingness to put their lives on the line in FBI tactical positions.

Maggie shrugged, swiping a hand over her face that completely missed the smear of camouflage paint left along her hairline. "Doesn't matter. I have a date with my TV and a bowl of popcorn tonight."

That was Chelsie's evening plan, too. She smiled at her friend, who'd been with the Washington Field Office's SWAT team for the past four years. SWAT was an ancillary position, meaning Maggie did that in her spare time. She spent her days as a regular Special Agent working civil rights cases like hate crimes and human trafficking. She was in the thick of it all the time, while Chelsie had come back to the WFO a year ago and not only dropped hostage negotiation but switched to the safest job she could find. White-collar crime, where lives were rarely on the line. Where she wouldn't have to stand by and watch while nine people were shot and killed.

Chelsie shuddered and Maggie eyed her questioningly.

As the days had turned into months, she'd slowly stopped having nightmares about her only case as a negotiator. The FBI had found her not to have any fault in the incident. They'd cleared her within a week and expected her to continue as a negotiator. But Chelsie had wanted out. It was her job to change the outcome of cases like that. If she couldn't do it, she had no business being a negotiator.

Maggie knew about that day—it had been big news at the time. But Chelsie had never discussed it with her, especially not what had happened the night before with Maggie's older brother. The only one-night stand she'd had in her entire life.

And she certainly wasn't going to put any of that on Maggie now. Tomorrow was the anniversary of the shooting, but they'd caught the perp the same day. She'd testified against him, and his trial had finally concluded last month.

Clayton Connors was a former soldier, honorably discharged after suffering minor injuries in an IED that had killed the rest of his unit. It had seemed likely that his insanity plea would land him in a mental institution instead of prison, but after a week of deliberating, the jury had found him guilty. Chelsie had watched as he'd been led out of the courthouse in shackles, heading toward a maximum-security prison. He'd never be getting out.

The same couldn't be said for the man who probably still gave Maggie nightmares. Maggie had never shared her past with Chelsie, but she'd heard a few office whispers over the years. The Fishhook Rapist, who'd claimed one victim every September 1 before releasing her with a brand on the back of her neck, had started with Maggie a decade ago. It was when Maggie had been a senior in college, and Chelsie was certain it had led her friend to the FBI.

Maggie was a lot braver than she was. Instead of hiding behind the safest cases she could, she'd jumped into one of the roughest, and probably most dangerous, jobs in the Bureau.

Chelsie opened her mouth, wanting to ask Maggie how she did it, then promptly closed it. They'd bonded in the Academy as two of the few women in the class, but Maggie had come in with Ella Cortez, and theirs was a friendship Chelsie could never hope to match. She and Maggie shared stories in the office and got a beer together after work once in a while, but that was the extent of it.

She'd never told Maggie—or anyone else—the profound sense of failure she'd felt after the shooting. It had eroded her confidence to the point where her parents and three younger brothers had been certain she would quit the Bureau entirely. But somehow she'd stuck it out. Maybe one day, she'd feel like she belonged here again.

Instead of saying any of that to Maggie, Chelsie put on her usual smile and waved as Maggie hopped into her car. Then she strode to the back of the parking structure where she'd left her trusty old compact. Her steps slowed as she approached.

Beside her little car was a hulking black SUV.

And even from a distance, though she hadn't seen him in more than six months, she recognized the man standing beside it.

His hair was a little bit longer, not so close to a buzz cut as it had been a year ago. It was a little bit blonder, too, as if he'd been spending a lot of time in the sun. His deep brown eyes were covered with a pair of sunglasses, but she could still picture their exact shade. His expression was neutral, his jawline hard, but like always, he seemed to crackle with barely contained energy, seemed to exude charm just standing there. He looked as though he'd put on muscle, though she knew firsthand that his lanky form made him appear thinner than he actually was. When she'd taken off his clothes, she'd discovered muscles that had felt like steel under her greedy fingers.

She forced herself to keep moving, to stare at him with what she hoped was an expression as bland as his. She was five foot ten in flats and he still had half a foot on her. "Scott. What are you doing here?"

There was no question he'd been waiting for her. Anticipation fluttered to life in her stomach. He'd pursued her in those first few months after the shooting. He'd shown up at Shields or stopped by the WFO to see Maggie and then found a way to seek Chelsie out, too. He'd given her that sexy smile, and asked her to dinner, or out for drinks. Eventually, she'd said *no* enough times that he'd stopped chasing her.

She'd been shocked that he'd wanted even a second night. Chelsie had heard about some of his exploits through Maggie over the years, so she knew Scott had a reputation as a one-date kind of guy.

One-night stands had never been her style. But that night, she simply hadn't been able to resist him. She'd been on such an incredible high when she walked into Shields. She'd finally become an FBI negotiator and she'd wanted to celebrate. None of her usual friends at the office had been available, so she'd gone by herself. She'd expected to grab a beer and toast her accomplishment, then go home.

Then Scott had sat down next to her and bought her that beer. Out of all the women in there, Scott had turned the full force of his charm on her. The sexy, lopsided grin; the intensity of his gaze focused solely on her; the feel of his fingers brushing over hers—it had hit her with a longing she'd never felt. They'd stayed until closing time, long past when all the other agents had left.

When he'd invited her home, she'd planned to say no. But somehow, she'd stared into his deep brown eyes and found herself nodding, her heart beating faster as she'd told him to lead the way. She'd followed him out of that bar before she could change her mind.

Until this moment she hadn't realized how much she'd missed him.

She tried to forced back the emotion, tried to ignore the little voice in her head telling her it could have worked, if only she'd given him a chance. Scott might have chased after her, but he'd just wanted a repeat of that incredible night, a simple fling. It would have ended quickly, but inevitably someone would have found out. That wouldn't have made a dent in his career, but it sure would have hurt hers.

She didn't date other agents. As a woman, that was a quick way to make everyone around her question how she'd succeeded in the Bureau. She didn't need that.

Especially since it had happened once before. She hadn't gone out on a single date with her supervisor back in LA, but he'd shown interest, and that fast, the rumors had started. It had taken a transfer to Washington, DC to stop them. That romance would have been forbidden. One with Scott wasn't—they didn't work on the same squad. But she didn't want to risk it—her career or her heart. Not for someone who wasn't searching for anything remotely serious.

She'd known serious wasn't Scott's style the

second she'd met him, years ago, when she'd been out at a pub with Maggie and Ella and a few other agents. He'd swung by their table, said hello, his gaze lingering longer on the female agents, then he'd been off. He hadn't paid her any special attention then, but she'd definitely noticed him. She'd realized right away that it was probably better he hadn't homed in on her, because she didn't do casual. And it had been immediately obvious that casual was the only way he worked.

It didn't matter how her pulse picked up at the thought of him, even a year after their one incredible, spontaneous night together. It didn't matter how completely in tune his sense of humor had been with hers, how strangely comfortable she'd felt with him, how right his body had felt pressed against hers. It didn't matter how much she'd wished things had turned out differently. Because the truth was, he reminded her too much of a day she wanted desperately to forget, reminded her too much of her failure.

She tried to keep her face impassive, wishing she had her own shades to cover eyes that were probably showing too much as she stared up at him. Had he decided to try again? Was she crazy to keep resisting him?

His biceps flexed as he reached up and removed his sunglasses, and that fast, Chelsie's shoulders dropped. There was no heat in his eyes, just cool professionalism. If there was a hint of something more intimate lurking in those chocolate-colored depths, he hid it well.

"Chelsie." Scott's deep voice was flat and even, nothing like the way he'd growled her name as he'd lowered himself on top of her. His mouth had caressed hers exactly right, with a familiarity he shouldn't have known. His hands had slid over her body with a similar confidence, making her writhe beneath him desperately.

She swallowed hard, trying to banish the memory, and saw recognition flicker in his eyes, and couldn't hold his stare.

If Scott Delacorte had known exactly how to touch her, it wasn't because they were somehow magically in tune. It was because he had a lot of practice. Chances were he'd long since moved on. If she couldn't seem to do the same, she at least needed to do a better job of pretending.

Gritting her teeth, she tried to hide her reaction and looked back into his eyes.

His blank expression had cracked, letting a hint of what she'd seen in his eyes a year ago peek through. But his voice was hard and urgent as he demanded, "I need you to get in the SUV and come with me."

"What? Why—"

"Connors escaped from jail this morning. We're putting you in protective custody."

As SCOTT SPED out of the WFO's parking structure, he sensed Andre's gaze on him from the passenger seat. They'd been partners since Scott joined HRT. When you've put your life in someone else's hands enough times, spent enough missions scouting out targets for days on end, you got to know the person. Andre definitely knew something was up.

Scott had never told him about Chelsie. He wasn't the type to kiss and tell in general, but he wasn't completely secretive, either. Still he'd never spoken to anyone about what he'd shared with Chelsie. Somehow, it felt too intimate, and he wanted to lock the memory away, keep it only for himself.

From the backseat, Chelsie finally spoke up. "How'd he get out?"

"Faked a medical emergency," Scott said. "The ambulance was in a car crash. Connors overpowered his guard and then tackled the driver. He was gone before the police arrived."

Andre turned in his seat, stretched his hand toward Chelsie. "Special Agent Andre Diaz. Scott and I are partners at HRT."

"Chelsie Russell. So, Andre, why the protective custody?"

Tension vibrated in her voice. As an agent,

she was well aware they wouldn't put her into protective custody simply because a criminal from one of her cases had escaped.

"There was a break-in at your apartment this afternoon, about an hour after Connors got out," Andre said in his typical straightforward way.

"What? Why didn't anyone call me?"

"There's probably a message on your phone," Scott said. "You were in a meeting."

Scott sensed Chelsie lean forward in the backseat, and he couldn't help but notice the familiar scent of her strawberry shampoo. He wanted to reach his hand back and clasp it around hers, but he swallowed the urge and tightened his grip on the steering wheel instead. She might still have been attracted to him on some level— he'd seen that in her wide blue eyes the second she'd stepped close to him in the WFO parking lot—but Chelsie had made her feelings about him clear.

"Did he take anything? And how did he find me?" Chelsie asked.

"Well, the place wasn't ransacked," Scott answered. "We don't know how he tracked you down." Her information was unlisted, but apparently Connors's skills extended beyond his rifle.

"Are you sure it was Connors?"

"No. But prison officials went through Connors's cell after he got out and it seems like the guy was fixated on you." Scott gritted his teeth, remembering the briefing the team had gotten from Froggy an hour ago. The Bureau wanted Chelsie Russell in protective custody, and since Connors had gotten his marksman training from the military, they wanted a pair of snipers watching her.

HRT did protective details all the time. Protecting another agent was an unusual assignment, but Scott had volunteered. Every time he thought about Connors, he remembered how the man had shot the tactical mirror out of his hand from two hundred yards away. There were top-notch snipers in HRT, but this was Chelsie's life they were talking about. Regardless of her feelings for him, *he* had to be the one protecting her. And Andre, good friend that he was, had immediately raised his hand, too, when Scott volunteered.

"He fixated on me, how?" Chelsie asked, her voice tight.

"Your name was written repeatedly in a notebook that was found in his cell," Andre said. "He had limited internet privileges and when they checked, they discovered that he'd been looking for information on you."

At Connors's murder trial, the prosecuting attorney had argued the only reason the two community-center workers and Chelsie had lived was because Connors hadn't been able to line up shots on them. He'd been drawn to the site because of the military connection, but for some reason, after his capture, he'd become obsessed with Chelsie.

The FBI wasn't sure why he'd fixated on her—she'd barely arrived on scene before Connors had taken off. Maybe it was because, unlike the community-center workers, who'd been inside the building when he'd started shooting and who he might never have known were there, Chelsie had talked to him. Whatever she'd said must have made an impression. Or maybe it was just because she was the only one he'd known was there whom he hadn't been able to hit.

Apparently now he'd decided to come back and finish what he'd started. The two community-center workers had been put under protective custody, too, but the locals were handling that. And they'd only found references to Chelsie in Connors's cell.

"He won't get anywhere near you," Scott promised, and he knew there was no way anyone in the car could miss the too-personal conviction in his voice.

Andre's eyes flicked to him, then away, as the car went briefly, uncomfortably silent.

The silence stretched until finally Chelsie asked, "Where are we going?" Her voice was neutral, but she was trying too hard to sound as though she hadn't noticed his intensity.

The scent of strawberries faded as she leaned back in her seat, away from him.

"We're taking you to a safe house," Andre answered. "There's a bag for you in back. We had one of the cops who responded to the break-in pack it for you."

"A female cop," Scott added, ridiculously bothered by the idea of a male cop pawing through her underwear drawer. An equally ridiculous thought followed—the hope that the cop had packed the underwear set Chelsie had been wearing when they were together. Pale pink and completely, unexpectedly feminine, especially underneath the straight-cut dress pants and loose button-down she'd worn to Shields.

"Okay," Chelsie said, obviously having no idea about the direction of his thoughts.

But from the way Andre's lips were quivering, he had an idea. When Scott glanced at his friend, Andre's eyebrows lifted toward the dome of his shaved head.

Ignoring him, Scott turned onto a random side street, weaving his way leisurely through the neighborhood and keeping an eye on the rear-view mirror.

"No one," Andre said as they came out the other side and Scott made a series of sudden, erratic turns.

They didn't have a tail. Good. There was no reason to think they'd been followed, but Scott wasn't taking any chances. Finally, he got back on the freeway and started driving south.

Ironically, the safe house was only fifteen miles from his home, ten miles from the scene of the shooting. It was in the middle of nowhere, an abandoned farmhouse on a flat, empty piece of land that would telegraph anyone's approach for miles. No good place for a sharpshooter to set up a hide, which was the reason they'd chosen it.

He and Andre had driven over there right

after the briefing and set the place up, leaving Andre's car behind. Then they'd gone back for Chelsie. Good thing they'd been fast because although a message had been left for Chelsie not to leave the office, apparently it hadn't been delivered.

Hopefully, they'd catch Connors quickly and lock him behind bars again, and Chelsie would be safe. She could go back to her white-collar cases at the WFO and he could go back to pretending he didn't miss her.

But as she leaned forward again, and he took a deep breath of strawberry—his new favorite scent—Scott revised that thought. Hopefully Connors would stay on the run long enough for Scott to change Chelsie's mind about giving him another chance.

THE SAFE HOUSE looked a lot like Scott's cozy little bungalow.

As soon as Chelsie stepped through the door, she halted, making Scott walk into her.

He gripped her arm quickly, before she stumbled, and the feel of his strong fingers wrapped around her elbow sent goose bumps running up her arm. The heat of his body against her back made her want to lean into him and hook her arms around his neck. Instead she jerked forward out of his grasp, and put some distance between them.

Not glancing back, she stepped farther into the house, and tried to cool down. It had been a year! And they'd only spent one night together. An incredible night, but still… How could he still affect her like this?

It was ridiculous. He wasn't her type at all. She didn't go for the too-handsome, too-charming playboy types. She dated accountants and engineers, decent looking but not so attractive that every woman in the room stared. They were safe and serious. She picked the ones who didn't feel threatened by her job because they believed her when she said she sat behind a desk. Guys who wanted more than a little fun and a little fling.

"I'm going to catch a nap." Andre's voice broke into her thoughts and she turned to face him. "Scott and I were called in for a case about—" he checked his watch "—eighteen hours ago."

"Sure, okay," she said, and silently cursed at how nervous she sounded. Hopefully Andre would think it was just the situation, and not the thought of being alone with Scott.

Scott's partner nodded at her, his dark brown eyes unreadable as he moved past her toward one of the bedrooms, a duffel bag slung over one shoulder and a tactical bag hanging from his other hand. He was undeniably attractive, probably in his early thirties and about her height, with smooth, dark skin, and biceps that strained his T-shirt.

As Andre disappeared into the room at the end of the hall, closing the door with a soft thud, Chelsie glanced back to find Scott watching her. He, too, had a duffel bag over one shoulder, and a tactical bag over the other. And, she realized, a small blue duffel bag tucked beside the tactical bag. Her belongings.

She held out a hand for it. "Sorry. I can take that."

Scott gave her the bag, his fingers brushing hers…on purpose? The same sensitivity rushed up her skin, the feeling of him lingering after he'd stepped back.

"Why don't you go ahead and settle in?" He tossed the car keys on the table and put his bags down. "I'm going to make a quick phone call and then I want to review the case file."

Chelsie nodded mutely as her stomach churned. After her testimony at Connors's trial had concluded, she'd hoped she'd never have to see anything from that horrible day again. Even thinking about the case made the memories rush back, the metallic scent of blood floating on the wind, the heat of the sun beating down on her shoulders, the bang of the rifle as another man fell and nothing she said made any difference.

She turned away from Scott, hoping he wouldn't see the emotions on her face, and walked down the hallway to another bedroom. Once inside, she shut the door and leaned against it, glancing around as her heart rate slowed. The shades were drawn on the room's sole window, and she'd keep them that way. The room was simple: a single bed, a nightstand and a dresser, all mismatched. A dusty treadmill sat in the corner with an ancient radio propped on top of it.

She set her duffel on the bed, not bothering to see what the cop had packed for her, and sank down beside it. The springs on the bed sagged too far under her weight as she stared at the blank walls.

The bones of the house really were a lot like Scott's little bungalow. But Scott's house had been full of charm and personality. For a guy with a reputation with the women, she'd expected a true bachelor's pad: leather couches, a big-screen TV and a black bedspread on a king-size bed. Instead, she'd discovered his taste in decorating ran to blues and greens. He had artwork on his walls, family pictures on his tables and his bedroom could only be described as cozy.

She'd been in his house just once. And most of those hours had been spent in his bed. So why could she picture it better than some of her friends' houses that she'd been to dozens of times?

"I don't know how long I'll be gone." Scott's voice suddenly carried into her room, loud enough for her to overhear.

He must have gone into the third bedroom, had to be on the phone. With a girlfriend? Was Scott Delacorte actually dating someone seriously enough that she might miss him if he was away for a few days? Heck, for all she knew, he was living with someone.

Chelsie pushed the thought out of her mind. It was none of her business.

Still, she couldn't help straining to listen as he added, "Keep an eye on her, okay?" He sounded stressed, as though whoever needed looking after was someone he didn't want to leave alone. As though he wanted to be the one watching over her.

Did he resent being sent to a safe house to watch over Chelsie instead?

Stop it, Chelsie told herself. Scott had given her plenty of opportunities to be with him. She'd been the one to say *no*. She had no right to be jealous of whoever had his attention now.

But as she heard Scott say goodbye to whoever he'd called, she knew it didn't matter what she told herself to feel. The truth was, she hadn't been able to stop thinking about Scott in the past year. But he wasn't a real option, just a momentary distraction, and she needed to deal with it. She stood, squared her shoulders, and went to the door, yanking it open.

Scott was standing on the other side, his hand raised as though he'd been about to knock. He slowly lowered his arm as she stared up at him.

And then, before she could move, he'd taken a step forward, until he was standing so close to her that she could see his eyes darken and his pupils expand. And then his head lowered toward hers.

He moved slowly, giving her time to step away, but she couldn't seem to break his spell. And then she was the one moving toward him, pushing herself up on her tiptoes and threading her fingers in his hair.

His mouth came down hard on hers, his lips urgent and so familiar. She sighed in the back of her throat as she pulled him closer. He wrapped his arms around her, kissing her again and again, until she felt as if she had been transported backward a year.

As if the massacre had never happened. As if she'd gone home with him from Shields—the only truly spontaneous, irresponsible thing she'd ever done—and just stayed. As if this was the beginning of something, instead of long past the end.

The thought brought her abruptly back to reality. She untangled her hands from Scott's hair and pushed against his chest as he was walking her backward, toward that single bed. She pushed a little harder and his lips left hers.

His gaze was intense, but as he stared at her, all trace of emotion disappeared. He stepped back abruptly, making her stumble, and his lips hooked up at the corner derisively. "Still playing games with me, Chelsie?" His voice seemed to caress her name, but the expression on his face was one of disgust. At her? At himself? She wasn't sure.

But when he turned and walked out of her room, she didn't call him back.

Chapter Three

"You want to take a look at this?" Scott asked as Chelsie finally emerged from the bedroom.

He was set up at the old pine table in the kitchen, his laptop in front of him, and the file from the police station in DC open. He didn't move his gaze from the screen as her footsteps slowly came toward him.

She stopped behind him, leaning over his shoulder, and a strand of soft blond hair brushed his arm before she tucked it away. "What is it?"

Her tone was wary, as if he'd been at fault for what had happened in her room fifteen minutes ago. But there was no way he'd have been able to *not* kiss her, the way she'd been staring up at him, longing in her big blue eyes.

He didn't know what her game was. A year ago, she'd been anxious to come home with him. And, okay, she'd made it clear afterward that she wanted nothing more from him. But as soon as he'd seen her in the WFO parking lot, she'd broadcasted her desire like it was a neon sign.

He was only human. And she was the only woman he hadn't been able to get out of his mind after he'd had her in his bed.

He'd tried hard, though, in the past six months. He'd gone from one fling to the next as though he was going for a record. And he was tired of it. One deep breath of Chelsie's shampoo and he was right back where he'd been a year ago.

What had he been thinking, volunteering for this gig?

Scott moved to the side, so she could see his screen. A picture from inside her apartment living room filled his monitor.

She gasped and leaned closer. "What is this?"

"The cops who were called to the break-in took them. I asked them to email me the pictures so you could see if anything obvious was missing." He twisted in his seat so he could look up at her, careful to keep his emotions off his face.

Bent down to scrutinize his computer screen, she was only a few inches away, her knee pressed against his leg. When she turned to him, her face was close to his and her pupils were huge.

He couldn't help but smile. She wasn't as immune to him as she wanted him to think.

Chelsie frowned, returning her eyes to the screen. "Not that I can see."

Scott reached forward and clicked to the next image, this one a picture of her bedroom. The walls were a pale pink, her bedspread a thick, puffy white down, and there was actually a vanity with perfumes and jewelry in the corner. It was unbelievably girly, not at all what he'd expected Chelsie's bedroom to look like.

Did she actually wear perfume and jewelry? Certainly not at the office, unless he counted the small gold locket she'd been wearing a year ago and had on now, paired with a crisp black blouse and wide-cut gray pants. Was there some lucky guy she actually changed out of her figure-hiding work clothes for, some lucky guy that made her dab on perfume and slip into a slinky dress?

He tried to ignore the thought and asked, "How about here?"

She shuffled her feet and her cheeks went red beneath the curtain of wheat-blond hair. Apparently she didn't like him peering into her private life, into the apartment where she'd never invited him. "I don't think so."

He opened a few more pictures—her kitchen, her bathroom, even inside her closets—but each time, she shook her head.

He shrugged. "Worth a try. The cops didn't

think he messed with anything. The neighbors might have scared him off."

"Or since I wasn't home, there was nothing else that interested him," Chelsie countered.

Scott nodded slowly. "It's possible."

Though as a trained marksman, the reality was, Connors could have set up on the roof of the apartment building across the street and waited for her to come home, then picked her off as soon as she got out of her car. Had he chosen to break in instead because he was on the run and couldn't risk waiting? Or was it because he wanted to do more than just kill her?

Either way, Scott was grateful Connors had made that mistake, because it had forced the Bureau to act, to get Chelsie to safety.

"What are you thinking?" Chelsie asked.

He shook his head, not wanting to scare her. It didn't matter what Connors was after; he wasn't going to find it now.

"Scott…" Chelsie fiddled with her locket, avoiding his gaze. "About before…"

"Yeah?"

She scowled, finally looking into his eyes.

She'd probably wanted him to jump in, to say he understood, that it was a mistake, that it wouldn't happen again. But he wasn't going to make it so easy. Her feelings about him might be running cold right him now, but he had a feeling she'd swing hot again sooner or later. And when that happened, there was no way he'd be turning her down.

Chelsie flushed, as if she could read his mind, and stammered, "I—I think we need to forget about our history, okay? I'm sure Connors will be caught soon. And then you can get back to whatever you want to be doing right now."

She didn't know he'd volunteered to be on her protective custody detail? Instead of telling her, he turned back to his laptop. "Let's go over the case file from last year."

"What?" Chelsie jerked backward. "Why?"

He frowned up at her. "Because it might give us something useful."

"What could it possibly give us?"

Scott narrowed his eyes, taking in the tight line of her lips, the furrow in her forehead, the clenching of her jaw. She didn't want to see the pictures, he realized suddenly.

He understood it. He didn't particularly like viewing crime-scene photos himself. But it went with the job. And Chelsie might have switched to white-collar crime, but he knew she'd started in counterterror. She'd probably seen photos of much worse.

Was it because she'd been there? He'd heard part of her testimony at Connors's trial. He knew she'd tried to talk him down. But she'd arrived on the scene about sixty seconds before he killed everyone except her. Not exactly enough time to establish a connection and start up a dialogue. Not enough time to change his mind, or stall him until HRT could take him down.

As a trained negotiator, she should have known that. There were some personalities who were hell-bent on killing, and no dialogue, no matter how well thought out, could stop it. And this type of killer—a spree shooter—was usually one of them.

Most of them actually planned on dying themselves before the day was done, either by self-inflicted gunshot or "suicide by cop." Connors might have had that plan in mind, too, but when he'd gotten the chance to run, he'd taken it. And when he'd been caught at a roadblock later that day, rather than lift the rifle lying across his lap, he'd been too cowardly to take his own life. Instead, he'd lifted his hands and stepped slowly out of his car.

"It wasn't your fault, Chelsie," Scott said softly.

"Of course not," she replied, but he could tell she didn't believe it.

"Is that why you stopped being a negotiator?" He'd known it was the Connors case, but he'd thought it was the reality of having to stand that close to the line of fire and watch people get killed. He'd thought it was the stress of it, the horror of seeing all that bloodshed up close and personal. Until now, he'd never suspected she'd blamed herself for any of it.

"Nothing from that day is going to reveal where Connors is now," she said, sidestepping his question.

Scott stood and Chelsie moved away from him, looking wary.

"Come on, Chelsie. You can't blame yourself for Connors's actions."

"I don't," she snapped, putting a hand up when he moved toward her. "I don't want to talk about this with you, Scott. And I don't think review-ing old crime-scene pictures is going to make any difference. There must be a state-wide APB out on Connors. They'll catch him and we can both go home."

She turned and hurried to her room before he could reply.

Scott sat back in his seat, staring blankly at his laptop. That was a lot of baggage to carry around—the deaths of nine military officers who'd left behind wives, children and, in one case, grandchildren.

In HRT, Scott had seen too many people die. It came with the job that sometimes by the time they could act, lives had already been lost. But it comforted him to know how many more were saved.

A sudden fury hit him. Connors had taken more than Scott had realized on that beautiful June day. Not only had he robbed nine men of their lives, he'd also stolen away a promising career.

Scott might not have seen Chelsie in action, but he'd heard enough about her from Maggie and some of the other agents at the WFO long before he'd taken her home. Even before she'd trained as a negotiator, she'd had a reputation as someone who could see to the heart of what a perp wanted and talk him into choosing a peaceful way to get it.

It was not a talent a lot of people had. He sure

didn't. He could take out a moving target at half a mile, but talking down a terrorist with a bomb strapped to his chest? That was a job he'd gladly leave to someone else.

Cursing under his breath, Scott pulled up the case file from last year. Chelsie might not want anything to do with it, but there was something about this whole situation that felt off to Scott. Something about Connors's actions that didn't add up. And the answer had to be in the original case, or in the trial testimony.

Wherever it was, he planned to find it. And hopefully, it would lead them to Connors.

Once they put Connors back behind bars where he belonged, Scott could turn to the next problem. And suddenly that wasn't how to get Chelsie back in his bed, but how to convince her not to throw away her career as a negotiator.

And if she happened to fall for him again in the process, he wasn't going to put up a fight.

FEAR PUMPED THROUGH Chelsie's veins as she crouched outside the community center, pressed as tightly to the brick wall as possible. The roar of the rifle was all she could hear. Dead men lay in the parking lot, their blood slowly streaming toward her.

Her bullhorn was discarded across her lap, useless, as somewhere out there, Connors tried to center her skull neatly in his crosshairs. Chelsie crouched lower. Everyone was dead. She was a failure, a failure, a failure…

Bang!

The sound split through the air as Chelsie jolted upright, breathing too hard. Everything was dark, except for the light streaming toward her from the left, and it took her a minute to get her bearings, for her eyes to adjust.

She was in the bedroom in the safe house. She'd been sleeping, having the dream again— the one she thought she'd quit having six months ago. She wasn't back at the community center with Connors trying to kill her. It was over.

She was safe. As long as Connors didn't find her again.

Scott stood in the open doorway, backlit from the hall. He held a laptop in his hands and his hair was sticking up on top. He seemed exhausted, but there was a sharpness to his expression that made her drag the covers up to her chin.

Which was ridiculous, since the cop who'd been called to the break-in at her apartment had packed her a conservative T-shirt and pajama shorts to sleep in. Scott had already seen her naked, already had his hands and mouth on just about every inch of her skin.

"What are you doing in here?" she croaked, glancing at the clock on the nightstand. She'd gone to bed hours ago, after eating a silent, awkward dinner with Scott. She'd thought he was asleep, too. Andre had woken up to finish off the rest of the cold pizza and take the next watch.

"I knocked," Scott replied. "You okay?"

"Fine." As he stepped into her room and flicked on the light, Chelsie squinted up at him. "Did they find Connors?"

"Not yet."

She slumped against the headboard, dropping her covers. "Then what do you want?"

His gaze slid over her, and she squirmed as he moved closer, his steps slow and sure. His jeans and T-shirt fit his lanky body just right, made him seem laid-back and approachable while doing nothing to hide the bunching muscles underneath. It reminded her of how he'd looked in Shields a year ago.

It reminded her of exactly why she'd thrown thirty-four years of caution away and gone home with a near-stranger.

In a lot of ways, he was still a stranger. They'd talked in Shields, had discovered they could make each other laugh, that they had similar outlooks on their jobs. But once they'd left the bar, they hadn't exactly passed the hours chatting. She could describe the birthmark on his upper thigh in minute detail, but she couldn't say if he had any siblings besides Maggie, what he'd done before he'd joined the Bureau or how he spent his free time.

As he sat on the edge of her bed, sinking down on the springs, his weight shifting her closer to him, an ache filled her chest. She wished she did know those things. Maybe it wasn't too late. She opened her mouth, wanting to ask him... something, but he spoke first.

"I want you to check out the crime-scene images."

Chelsie sat up straighter, moving away from him as he held his laptop toward her. "What? Why? No."

She sounded frantic, but she didn't care. The nightmares were already starting up again. She didn't need to study the crime-scene photos and make it worse, regardless of how much of a coward that made her seem.

She scowled, hating that Scott would see her that way now, too. He'd picked a job where he ran into the danger everyone else ran away from. He'd already seen her run away, from her job as a negotiator, and from him.

Steeling herself, she grabbed the laptop before she could change her mind. But there were no crime-scene photos on his screen, only a drawing with the details—distances, locations of the victims and the shooter—written in. Surprised, she glanced over the top of the screen at Scott.

He moved slightly, leaning against the headboard, and stretched his long legs across her bed.

There wasn't enough room for both of them, and she found her legs pressed against his through the thin sheet, with nowhere to go. If she turned her head, raised it a little, his face would be right there. His lips would be right there.

Instead, she stared resolutely at the screen. "What am I looking at?" Her voice sounded too high-pitched, but if Scott noticed, he didn't say anything.

Instead, he pointed to the spot on the drawing marked *Suspect*. "Connors was here." He moved his finger to the spot right outside the community-center front door. Next to an X, it read *FBI Special Agent Russell*. "You were here?"

There was a tension in his voice she didn't understand. "Yeah." She glanced at him, and this close, she could see the individual whiskers on his chin, the tense lines between his eyes that she wanted to smooth.

"Not here?" He moved his finger from the left side of the U outside the community-center front door to the right side.

"No. Why?"

"Chelsie." The worry in his voice deepened, and there was concern in the depths of his deep brown eyes. "Connors not firing at you wasn't because he couldn't."

Chelsie's pulse picked up. "What are you talking about?"

"Look where he is." He pointed to the X marked *Suspect* again.

"So?"

"So, I ran the numbers. If they're right, he *did* have a shot at you. He chose to let you live. He chose to let *only* you live."

Chapter Four

Chelsie stared up at Scott, uncomprehending. "What do you mean, he *let* me live?"

"He had a shot, Chelsie," Scott said quietly. "We found his shell casings. He was high enough on those bleachers. He could have hit you."

"If that's true, then why didn't he?" Chelsie demanded, not wanting to believe it. "If he could have gotten me in his crosshairs, he would have killed me. He snapped. He was taking out anyone he could hit that day."

"Apparently not," Scott said.

She stared at him, noticing the deep circles

underneath his eyes. Andre had said they'd been up for eighteen hours before they'd brought her to the safe house. And yet, instead of getting some sleep, Scott had reviewed the case file.

Chelsie felt something suspiciously like affection, and tried to ignore it. "Maybe you did the geometry wrong."

Scott shook his head, but instead of being insulted, he just appeared exhausted. "It's the same kind of calculations I do in my head every time I fire my rifle, Chelsie. I mess those up and I shoot a hostage instead of the perp. I could do them in my sleep. Trust me. I'm not wrong."

"Then why didn't they figure this out before?" she demanded.

"If you look at the building from ground level, you'd assume he didn't have an angle on you. Even if you look at it from the bleachers, if you'd been on the other side of that enclosed area, he wouldn't have been able to hit you. It was an oversight. And it made sense that he didn't hit you because he couldn't. But that's not what happened."

"Then what was he really after?" she whispered, moving away from him on her bed. But the mattress offered no support and she just slid back toward him until her body was pressed against his again.

It didn't make any sense. Clayton Connors had been suffering from post-traumatic stress disorder after watching the rest of his unit die when an IED exploded under their vehicle. He'd gotten out of the military and gotten help—mostly in the form of very strong painkillers. Then, one day, he'd snapped and gone after military recruiters.

But the prosecution at his trial had made an airtight argument that Connors would have killed anyone he could have hit that day, that he'd actually planned on moving to a new location and killing again, until he'd been pulled over. It had been simple self-preservation that had kept him from raising a gun on the officers.

A sudden fear of dying himself had landed him in jail instead of the morgue.

Chelsie threw her covers off and walked to the far side of the room. She crossed her arms over her chest, feeling strangely exposed in her T-shirt and shorts as she stared down at Scott, who was way too tempting stretched out in her bed. "The guy was crazy. Does it really matter why he didn't shoot me?"

Even as she asked the question, she knew she was avoiding dealing with it. Connors letting her live on purpose didn't fit with anything they knew about what had happened that day. And it didn't track with the idea of him coming after her for a second chance, not if he'd never taken that first chance.

So what did he want with her? A shiver ran through her and she tensed, hoping Scott wouldn't notice.

He put the laptop on her bed and walked over to her, stopping so close that she could've leaned forward and rested her head on his chest.

"You're the one who gets into people's minds," he argued. "You tell me if it matters."

"That would be Ella. She's the profiler."

Scott gave her a look of disbelief. "Oh, come on. You were a good negotiator because you understand what people want. How did you do that without getting into their minds?"

"In case you forgot, I failed as a negotiator."

"That's not true," Scott said. "Connors was a nutbag. You couldn't have talked him down if you had thirty days, let alone the thirty seconds you probably got."

She put her hands on her hips. "You just came in here to say that Connors *wasn't* a nutbag. That he'd made the conscious choice not to shoot me, instead of being driven by some blind rage."

Scott paused. It was a fraction of a second, but it was long enough.

"I don't want to talk about my old job," she said. "You're the one who's so sure he could have shot me. You must have far more experience with that kind of scene than I do. What's *your* assessment?"

Scott frowned back at her. "Remind me not to wake you without a full night's sleep again. You're seriously cranky without your coffee."

Chelsie's shoulders slumped, her anger deflating. He'd stayed up reviewing the case when she'd refused to study it, and he'd taken on her protective custody when he probably could have passed it off to someone else. It wasn't his fault talking about that day got her hackles up.

When she'd officially become an FBI negotiator, she thought she'd finally found her calling. Now, any reminder of her short-lived role in the specialty made every ounce of insecurity rise up. Including Scott. She'd probably never think about him without remembering the massacre, without remembering how she'd failed to prevent it.

She'd spent the past year trying to leave that memory in her past, and Scott with it.

Realizing that Scott was staring at her as

though trying to read what was going through her head, she evened out her expression. "Sorry. Let's talk about this in the morning then, after I get that coffee."

He gaped at her. "The Chelsie I remember would want to jump right in."

There was only one thing he would remember her jumping right into, and that was his bed. She scowled to hide her embarrassment, and snapped, "Don't fool yourself, Scott. You never knew me."

His eyes locked on hers, studying her too long, until she felt the need to fidget. "Maybe not," he finally said, "but I don't think I'm the one fooling myself right now." Before she could respond, he turned and walked out of the room.

When the door shut quietly behind him, Chelsie sank back onto the bed, feeling angry and sad and vaguely ashamed of herself. What was that supposed to mean? *She* was somehow fooling herself?

The laptop he'd left behind had slid toward

her as the mattress sank under her weight. She glanced at the screen, still lit up with the drawing of the community center's front parking lot.

If Scott was right—and as an HRT sniper, chances were, he was—then why hadn't she died with everyone else at that community center a year ago? And if Connors had let her live back then, why was he after her *now*?

"I'M SORRY."

Scott blinked at the light streaming in from the hallway, even though he'd been awake from the second Chelsie had started tiptoeing down the hall. She stood in the doorway of his bedroom, holding his laptop. She'd changed into a pair of jeans and a T-shirt—this time, unfortunately, with a bra underneath. She did seem contrite. She also looked uncomfortable. Because she didn't like to apologize or because he slept in nothing but boxer shorts, he wasn't sure.

After he'd left her room, he'd asked Andre to take over the watch, deciding to get some much-needed sleep. He'd figured by the morning, she'd have come to grips with what he'd shared. And hopefully she'd be less defensive.

Scott rubbed his eyes and yawned, making her apologize again. But not before she glanced at his bare chest and then quickly back up.

"It's okay."

He expected her to turn and go back the way she'd come, but instead she stepped farther into his room. She settled on the very edge of his bed, setting his laptop between them, like some kind of barrier.

"It's been a year. Why would he be after *me*? It's not like it was my testimony that put him away."

Scott pushed himself to a sitting position. Apparently they were talking about this now, after all. "You were the only eyewitness to the shootings, but—"

"But I never saw him! It wasn't like I could identify Connors as the shooter."

"What I was going to say," Scott cut in, "was

that I agree. You didn't do the most damage at his trial. With or without you, he was going down."

After Connors had been pulled over in a Taurus with a license plate matching the one HRT had called in from the scene of the shooting, the rifle on his lap had been tied to the shell casings at the scene. The physical evidence alone would have taken him down.

Add to it an incompetent public defender, Connors refusing to say a word in his own defense plus the families of the victims speaking at the sentencing, and Connors was going to jail. With or without the testimony of the one woman he'd let walk away from that massacre.

Chelsie crossed her arms over her chest, holding on to herself as if that could protect her from Connors, from what had happened that day.

And it made him wonder what had happened to her. To the strong, determined negotiator he'd brought home from Shields Tavern. He couldn't believe she'd let Clayton Connors take so much away from her.

But confronting her about it was guaranteed to get her guard up, so instead he said, "I think if we can figure out what he's after, it'll help us track him down."

"What does killing me now accomplish?"

"I don't know, Chelsie." Scott put his hand on her arm, and she flinched away. Trying not to let it bother him, he said, "But you're safe here."

She shook her head. "I'm not worried."

When she met his eyes again, he saw the truth of her statement on her face. She trusted him and Andre to keep her safe. It was better than nothing, but he wanted more. He wanted a heck of a lot more.

"Why do you think he never said a word in his own defense at his trial?" Chelsie asked, just when Scott was trying to figure out how to broach what had happened between them.

He forced himself to put his mind back on track. It didn't matter that the woman he'd been fantasizing about for the past year was finally back in his bed—though not in the way he wanted. He had a job to do here. And he couldn't let himself get distracted.

"What defense could he have possibly have given? I think he was banking on people feeling sorry for him because of the PTSD, and figured the insanity plea would work," Scott replied.

"I don't know," Chelsie argued. "Wouldn't he at least want to explain where he was coming from? He could've drummed up some sympathy. He was a war hero, after all. And he watched his entire unit die. The defense attorney talked about his PTSD, but Connors never spoke at all."

"I was only in the courtroom for part of the trial," he reminded Chelsie. He'd had to testify about his role in the day's events. He hadn't heard the attorney talk about the post-traumatic stress disorder, although obviously Connors had it. Still, Scott had known there was more going on. "Every time I saw Connors, he was pretty glassy-eyed. Whatever he was on must've been strong. Maybe his lawyer didn't want to risk putting him on the stand and have him make things worse."

"Still—"

"We need to focus on what his motivation is now," Scott cut in, holding back a yawn. He didn't care why Connors hadn't taken the stand a year ago; all he cared about was why the guy was after Chelsie now.

"Maybe he wants someone new to blame. A year ago, he blamed the military for his unhappiness. Now, he's decided it's my turn."

In Scott's opinion, it didn't fit, but then, he wasn't a negotiator. Or a profiler. "I'll give Ella a call tomorrow. See if she has any ideas."

"That's a good idea. Why don't we try now?"

"Chelsie." Scott glanced at the clock next to his bed. "It's after midnight."

"Ella's kind of a night owl, isn't she? She was at the Academy anyway."

"I'll call her tomorrow," Scott replied.

Chelsie didn't seem happy, but she nodded and stood. "Okay."

When she turned to go, Scott stopped her with, "Since we're talking motivation here, let me ask you something." He knew he shouldn't, but he had to know. "Why did you give Connors the power to drive you out of negotiation?"

She spun back around, and although he knew it had been a mistake to ask, he liked the fire suddenly sparking in her eyes. He'd rather have her fighting mad than spiritless.

Before she could argue, he added, "It's part of the gig. You can't win them all. It's not like you to give up so quickly."

"You don't know me," she said, taking a step closer, the muscles in her lean arms outlined, her jaw tight.

"You'll stand up to me," Scott said. "So why not for a job you obviously loved?" Trying another tactic, he asked, "I mean, what made you pick negotiation in the first place?"

He thought she was going to say it was none

of his business—or tell him where he could shove it—but instead she asked, "What made *you* pick the FBI? Huh?" She stepped closer, fury on her face, and he knew he'd crossed a line even before she added, "You want to talk about *your* motivation? You want to talk about what happened to Maggie?"

Scott got out of bed so fast that Chelsie backed up. It had been ten years since his sister's assault, the event that had driven him into the Bureau. And Chelsie wasn't the first person, or even the first FBI agent, to ask about it. But her throwing that at him pissed him off more than pretty much any other response she could have given.

Maybe that was the point, he thought as he got in her face and watched her eyes widen. No matter how she might want to deny it, she knew how to get inside people's minds. She was getting in his right now, trying to use his emotional weak spot to drive him away.

"Fine," he said, his voice barely above a whisper. "You want to push me away, Chelsie? Congratulations."

He pointed at the door. "Get out."

Chapter Five

What was wrong with her?

Chelsie walked slowly into the living room. She couldn't believe she'd thrown Maggie's assault in Scott's face. Even if Maggie hadn't been her friend, it was a horrible thing to do. Especially since Maggie's rapist was still out there somewhere, still claiming a new victim every year.

She'd seen Scott's expression as he'd asked her to dredge up all the memories from the day of the massacre. That determined expression that told her he'd push until he got what he wanted. The same intent look she'd seen that day back in the bar, when she'd taken his hand and let him take her to heaven.

And the idea of turning her psychoanalytic lens on herself, which she'd managed to avoid for a whole year, made her panic. So she'd done what came naturally. She'd figured out the one thing guaranteed to make him back away.

Scott was right about her. She *did* understand what people wanted. The flip side of that was, she was also good at figuring out what they *didn't* want, which for negotiations, was sometimes just as important.

So why *had* she failed that day? Accepting that she hadn't had time to make a difference was an easy excuse. Certainly there was some truth to it, but she, more than anyone, should have been able to connect with Connors. It might've been different if she'd known what he'd endured while serving, the loss of his unit. For a military long-timer like Connors, his unit would be his family.

And she understood that kind of loss. Her

stepmom was the only mother she remembered, but that was because her dad had married her when Chelsie was three. Her birth mom had been military, just like her dad. And she'd been killed on Chelsie's first birthday.

No matter that Chelsie didn't remember her. No matter that she had a close bond with her stepmom and half brothers. She still felt an empty space in her life, wishing she'd had the chance to know her mom.

If she'd seen Connors's military connection from the start, and used her own experience to forge a bond between them, he might have hesitated. Maybe even long enough for those men to run to her side, to safety.

Except that it hadn't really been safe, had it?

"Hi, Chelsie."

The sound of Andre's voice was a welcome distraction from thoughts that were headed in a direction she didn't like them to go.

She fingered the locket around her neck and nodded back at Andre, who was reading a book on the ugly brown plaid couch in the corner of the living room.

He set the book aside and gestured to the TV on the wall. "Can't sleep? You want to watch a show?"

Chelsie shook her head and sat down on the chair against the other wall, next to the side table where Scott had dropped the car keys when he'd come in the door. They were the only item on the table. Not that a safe house needed decorations, but it was a depressing place.

"I've been to worse," Andre said, apparently able to read the direction of her thoughts. "Hopefully we won't be here long. The FBI is putting a lot of resources on this. We'll find Connors." He spoke with the confidence of an agent who rarely failed.

Chelsie folded her legs underneath her on the chair and studied Scott's Bureau partner. Brooding was the best way to describe him. So different from Scott's laid-back attitude and easy grin. Despite Andre's bulky, muscle-heavy build, he looked a lot more like what she'd expect from a sniper: quietly observant.

It was a near certainty he'd noticed the history she and Scott shared, if he hadn't known it already.

"Have you and Scott been partners a long time?" The question came out unexpectedly, and Chelsie hoped it didn't sound like she was digging for information.

Andre's eyebrows rose slightly. "About a year and a half. Ever since he joined HRT."

Chelsie was surprised—Scott had only been on HRT for six months when he'd been called to the site of that massacre? The way he'd handled it, she'd thought he'd been on the team for years.

Andre stared at her expectantly, as if he was waiting for her to ask more about Scott, but instead she stood up. Instead of awkwardly pressing for details about Scott's life, she needed to figure out why there was suddenly a threat to *her* life.

"I need to make a call," she told Andre.

He glanced at his watch, then up at her. "It's one-thirty in the morning."

"It's okay. My brothers are in California. It's only ten-thirty there." It was true, but that wasn't who she was calling. Scott might want to wait until morning to call Ella Cortez, but Chelsie was pretty sure her friend would still be up.

Andre nodded and picked his book back up, but the way he watched her as she hurried out of the room suggested he knew she was lying.

Once she was in her bedroom with the door tightly shut, Chelsie used her personal phone to dial Ella, hoping she was right and her friend would still be awake.

Ella picked up on the second ring, and sounded far from sleepy when she answered.

"Ella? It's Chelsie Russell."

"Chelsie." She heard Ella partially cover the phone and say, "Hang on, Logan."

And then Chelsie remembered. She hadn't seen Ella in a several months and in that time, her friend had somehow met a police detective across the country and become engaged.

Chelsie shook her head at the idea. She'd had relationships last years and never come close to marriage. How did anyone know in a few months?

The thought made Scott's image rise up in her mind, but she ignored it. Her feelings for him had nothing to do with love, only lust.

"What's going on, Chelsie?"

Had Scott talked to Ella yet? Chelsie knew they were close; Scott and Maggie had grown up with Ella. But her friend didn't sound as though she knew Chelsie was in protective custody.

"Did you hear about Connors?" Chelsie asked carefully, not wanting Ella to know she was hiding away with Scott. Chelsie had failed as a negotiator, but Ella was a solid profiler. And a solid friend. Chelsie had a feeling if she so much as said Scott's name, Ella would somehow figure out their entire sordid history.

"I heard he's on the run," Ella replied. "But they've got BOLOs out on him across the whole county, so I doubt it'll be for long. Do you want a place to stay until they catch him?"

So, Scott hadn't told her yet. "No, thanks. I wanted your opinion on something, from a profiler's perspective."

"Shoot."

Chelsie winced at the innocent term. "Are you familiar with the case?"

"Familiar enough. What do you want to know?"

"I just learned that Connors had a shot at me that day and he didn't take it."

There was a short silence and then Ella said, "And you want to know why."

"Yes. Do you think it's because I was the only woman?"

"That's certainly possible," Ella said, but she sounded unconvinced.

"Because I was the only one not in the military?"

"That's more likely," Ella agreed, "but if that's

the case, then his spree was a lot more targeted than the FBI concluded. With a spree shooting like that, even if the perp is drawn to a place because of particular targets, he'll usually take out anyone else he sees—or at least anyone else who gets in his way. Which you were certainly trying to do."

"Well, what about—" Chelsie began, but Ella cut her off.

"He could have hit you before the HRT agents arrived? It wasn't about him choosing an escape rather than taking the time to line you up in his crosshairs?"

"He could have taken me out anytime."

"Hmm."

Chelsie was overcome by worry, by the fear that even Ella wouldn't be able to help her. And for some reason, Chelsie needed to understand why. More than just to figure out Connors's agenda now. She needed to know, because maybe it would help her come to terms with what had happened that day.

Why had she lived, when all the others had died? The man who'd been closest to her when he'd been hit had a one-year-old daughter waiting for him at home. He'd been shouting about his daughter as he'd made a run for Chelsie.

She grasped her locket. "It's important."

"Well, Logan just caught a case—he's a newbie here, which means he pulled the lousy shift. So I'm up now anyway. You want to take a ride and tell me about what happened that day?"

Chelsie glanced at her closed door. There was no way Scott or Andre would let her go anywhere. And she didn't have a particular desire to leave the safe house until Connors was caught.

Before she'd replied, Ella continued, "I need more information in order to really give you anything. And I'd like to see the crime scene myself."

"The community center?" She hadn't been back there since the shooting. The thought of returning there made a lump form in her throat.

"I want to see the layout—we can do it quickly

and then take off. I've got to work in the morning, but I'm up now anyway, and I won't be able to get to sleep until Logan is back," Ella said. "Connors is on the run, not skulking around the crime scene, hoping someone will happen by in the middle of the night. What do you say?"

When Chelsie didn't immediately answer, Ella joked, "I'll come armed if you do."

Chelsie took a deep breath, remembering the car keys on the table in the living room. Ella was right. If Connors was searching for her, he wouldn't be at the community center in the middle of the night. "I'll meet you there in twenty minutes."

AN ENGINE GUNNED to life, loud and too close.

Scott bolted out of bed and down the hall, through the open kitchen door. He found Andre standing outside, staring after Scott's SUV as it sped away from the drive.

Scott let out a string of curses and then turned to stare at his partner.

Andre scowled at the retreating SUV. "I got up to use the bathroom and Chelsie took your car keys and ran."

Scott cursed and looked down at his bare feet. "I'll be right back." He rushed to his room to throw on some clothes and his running shoes. He put his pistol in his holster and his tactical bag over his shoulder, then dashed back to Andre, who had his car running, the passenger door open.

Scott hopped inside. He barely had the door shut before Andre reversed into the road.

"Any idea where she's going?"

Andre shook his head as he hit the gas hard, moving in the direction Chelsie had disappeared. "She said she was going to call her brother, then she came out of her room and took off."

Chelsie had a brother? It suddenly hit him how little he really knew about her. "She called him at two in the morning?"

"She said her brothers live in California, so

it's earlier there. But she was lying. That's not who she was calling."

Scott didn't question Andre's assessment. He might not be a negotiator or a profiler, but he knew a *tell* when he saw one. *A profiler*, Scott realized. "She called Ella. She must be meeting Ella."

And Scott knew how Ella worked. She liked to see a crime scene up close, not hear about it over the phone or read about it in a case file. Chelsie must have decided to meet her. But why had she gone alone? Why hadn't she asked Andre to go or woken Scott? "She's going to the community center."

"You sure?" Andre asked.

"Yeah, I'm sure." Chelsie was impatient. It was a weird trait for a negotiator, who had to wait out suspects, sometimes for days. If she could keep a suspect talking, then he probably wasn't shooting. The idea was to talk him into surrender or, if necessary, distract him long enough for HRT or SWAT to go in.

Somehow, Chelsie managed to keep her impatient nature in check when she was on the job. But apparently not today.

Andre picked up speed, but Chelsie must have been rocketing down the country roads—or Scott was wrong about where she was going—because he didn't see his SUV.

"I can't believe she stole my car."

Andre snorted, probably to keep from telling Scott where he could shove it the next time he volunteered for a job like this. "I thought Chelsie *wanted* to be in protective custody until Connors was caught. I didn't realize I actually needed to babysit her."

"Neither did I," Scott replied through clenched teeth. "And I don't know what Ella was thinking, either."

"Did anyone inform her that Chelsie's in protective custody?"

"Probably not," Scott admitted.

"Well, at least she should be relatively safe.

It's not too likely Connors is going to be searching the middle of the countryside for her."

That much was true, but Scott still didn't like it. "Let's hurry anyway."

Andre gave the car more speed and Scott grabbed his cell phone, dialing Ella. The phone rang until it went to voice mail. Scott tried Chelsie, with the same result. Could he be wrong about where Chelsie was going? Or were they ignoring their phones for some reason?

"You ever going to share what your history is with this woman?" Andre asked, giving him a knowing grin as he rounded a bend.

"You remember a year ago when we all went out to Shields for Bobby's birthday?"

"Sure. He threw back so many shots that night that I took his keys and he slept in my bathtub."

"You wouldn't let him use the guest room?"

"Oh, I set him up in the guest room," Andre replied. "But the next morning, I found him passed out in my bathtub."

Scott shook his head, unable to imagine how

the six-foot-five, two-hundred-plus-pound Bobby had fit in anyone's bathtub. Though it did explain how his friend had gotten the nickname "Bathtub Bobby."

"Anyway, I met her that night, at Shields."

Realization flashed across Andre's face. "I *knew* she looked familiar, that day we showed up at the community center. She's the one you ditched us for the night before. You said you were leaving, then you were still there when the rest of us finally went home an hour later, chatting up a blonde in the corner. So, *that's* why you volunteered for this job."

"Yeah." Scott leaned forward in his seat, straining for any glimpse of his SUV. But aside from the clouds of dust swirling in Andre's headlights, indicating that someone had driven through recently, and way too fast, he didn't see much at all.

Andre shook his head, something like pity on his face. "Well, if it makes you feel any better, she was digging for details about you earlier."

"She was?" As soon as the words were out of his mouth, Scott cursed himself for how eager he sounded.

Andre laughed. "You're so screwed, my friend."

"Just drive," Scott said. He could finally see the community center up ahead, the back parking lot illuminated by dim bulbs, but the community center itself dark. His black SUV was parked near the back entrance, next to a little red Corvette he recognized as Ella's personal vehicle. But he didn't see Ella or Chelsie anywhere. And although he normally didn't mind the dark, tonight it felt ominous.

"They can't have beaten us here by much," Andre reminded him. "They're probably in the front, checking out the original scene."

Scott nodded his agreement, antsy as Andre stopped beside the vehicles. He got out of the car fast, his instincts humming. "I don't like this."

Nothing looked unusual, but Andre didn't

question his assessment. Instead, he jumped out of the car, his hand resting on his holster, instantly wearing the focused expression he always had when they arrived on scene for HRT.

It felt disturbingly like déjà vu as Scott raced alongside the community center, toward the front of the building. The last time he'd run along this little stretch, it had been to find a parking lot full of murder victims. Back then, he was racing after Chelsie, too.

This time, he sensed Andre close behind him, though he didn't hear him, either because Andre ran silently or because Scott couldn't hear anything over his heartbeat thundering in his ears. And this time, instead of checking around the corner with his tactical mirror first, he just rounded blindly. Logically, he knew everything was probably fine, but his gut was screaming something else entirely.

Standing in the center of the lot, deep in conversation, were Chelsie and Ella. Ella was wearing cargo pants and a tank top, her long, dark hair up in a messy ponytail, as though Chelsie's call had dragged her out of bed. Chelsie was in the same jeans and T-shirt she'd been wearing when she'd woken him up an hour ago. As soon as she spotted him, she'd probably be wearing the same pissed-off expression, too.

They'd been walking slowly toward the U-shaped entryway where Chelsie had been standing the day of the massacre, but when Scott rounded the corner, they turned toward him. Surprise flashed on Ella's face and guilt on Chelsie's. But they both looked fine.

Relief coursed through Scott. He glanced at Andre, who'd come up beside him and was scanning the area.

"Chelsie, what are you thi—" Scott started.

"Down!" Andre suddenly yelled. "Move!"

His partner was going for his Glock, but it was already too late, because Clayton Connors darted from the cover of the U-shaped entryway where he'd apparently been hiding.

Before Andre could get a lock on him, or Scott

had even cleared his pistol from the holster, Connors was standing directly behind Chelsie, holding a gun against her head.

Chapter Six

"Connors!" Scott shouted, moving left, hoping to get a better angle.

The man in him felt panic explode, seeing Chelsie used as a human shield, seeing Ella that close to a practiced killer.

Simultaneously, the seasoned sniper in him cataloged the space and the target. He couldn't help remembering the wide, open parking lot as it had been a year ago, smeared with the blood of Connors's first victims.

Connors himself was positioned close to Chelsie's back. He was dipped low so Scott couldn't take out his brain stem over Chelsie's head, something that would have dropped him instantly, no worries of him firing ever again.

Connors angled closer to Chelsie, moving right along with Scott, not letting him improve his angle, but not giving Andre a shot, either.

The guy knew what he was doing. Of course he did—the military had trained him well.

"Drop it!" Connors shouted. "All of you!"

Scott couldn't do it. He couldn't even consider it. He wasn't a negotiator. He was the tactical solution. And he couldn't provide that if he was unarmed and ten feet away from a gunman with a hostage.

But normally, Scott wouldn't be up against someone with Connors's skills, either. He'd read Connors's military personnel file, along with the case file. He was a decorated soldier, honorably discharged before he'd lost his mind and taken out a parking lot full of people. And he was one of the best sharpshooters the military had ever produced.

The kicker was the two women Scott loved, in

the crosshairs. Cared about, he corrected him-self. He loved Ella like a little sister and would never forgive himself if she was hurt because he'd misjudged a protective detail. As for Chel-sie...his feelings for her were too recent and untested to be love. But he couldn't fool him-self that it was only lust, either. He cared for her too much.

And he needed to focus right now so he could get both of them out of this mess alive.

Panic tightened in his chest as he slowly low-ered his weapon, but he didn't drop it. Still, the time it could take to raise his Glock if he needed to shoot could be too much. His rifle lay use-lessly in his tactical bag, heavy against his back.

Connors sounded too on edge. Scott couldn't drop the weapon, couldn't lose all tactical op-tions, but he had to lower the threat level for Connors, so he'd relax a little.

Beside him, Andre did the same and then Connors shifted toward Ella, who'd been slowly easing closer. "Don't even think about it," he snarled.

Ella raised her hands, her pistol still in its holster, and moved a step away, as Scott silently cursed. Tackling the gunman was a last resort—that close to Chelsie, he couldn't possibly miss. But Scott had known Ella since she was six years old, so he knew exactly how she worked. She approached tactical decisions with her profiler's mind—slowly, analytically and carefully. She wouldn't have taken a careless risk—and if he'd reacted faster and gotten Connors more effectively focused on him, she might have had a chance.

"Drop the guns," Connors enunciated slowly.

"You know we can't do that," Scott replied. Connors couldn't shoot Chelsie and have any hope of getting away, but in case he had delusions of doing that, Scott said carefully, "I'm HRT Agent Scott Delacorte. I think your unit trained with some of our guys a few years ago."

Connors made a sound somewhere between

disgust and frustration. "If you're trying to tell me you're almost as good a shot as I am, Scott Delacorte, I believe you. But don't try anything and you don't need to worry about it."

"What are you doing here?" Chelsie asked.

Her voice was calm and even, as though it was every day she had a gun pressed to her head by a convicted killer. Her eyes as they met Scott's were equally focused, but underneath lurked a torrent of emotions, and she glanced away before he could identify them all.

Her hands were positioned loosely by her sides, but bent enough at the elbows that Scott knew she had a tactical backup plan in mind. But if she hoped to pull her gun from her holster and hit Connors before he got her, she had to know it was probably the last thing she'd ever do.

It wouldn't come to that, Scott vowed.

"Your address book was very enlightening," Connors said, a tense undercurrent to his voice. "Who writes that stuff down anymore? But I'm glad you did." He paused, but didn't seem to notice as Scott inched painfully slowly to the right, as Andre eased a tiny bit left.

Andre was standing across from Ella. He'd have a hard time getting an angle on Connors between her and Chelsie. But Scott had worked with Andre long enough to recognize exactly what he was doing. Him moving away from Scott made more space for Connors to cover. They needed to get to a distance where Connors would need to move his head to see everyone—and they needed to do it without Connors realizing what was happening.

"I saw this one's name—" Connors jerked the gun briefly away from Chelsie's head to point it at Ella, then back again "—and looked her up. Lots of news stories about her from a few months ago, chasing down some serial killer, advertising that she's an FBI agent." He made a tsking noise, then added, "I tracked her down. It was easier than I would have expected for a Fed."

Ella paled, as both she and Scott realized Connors must have followed her here. Knowing Ella, she was blaming herself, but it was Scott's fault, not hers. He never should have let Chelsie out of his sight.

"Chelsie was just doing her job that day," Ella reminded him.

"Yeah, well, she was never my target," Connors snapped.

"I know," Chelsie replied. "You could have hit me from the bleachers. I appreciate that you didn't. Thank you."

Chelsie still avoided looking at Scott, but he saw approval in Ella's expression. Chelsie was trying to create a bond with Connors, get him to connect with her so he wouldn't be able to kill her.

It was actually really smart, trying to make Connors view the fact that he hadn't killed her a year ago as him saving her life. If he felt that, it would be harder for him to take that life now.

Scott understood the theory. But the reality

was, he'd been to too many shootings where the killer had every reason to feel bonded to his victims, and he killed them anyway.

By FBI protocol, tactical was always the last option. The primary goal was to protect any civilians, next to protect the lives of fellow agents, then to protect the life of the suspect. Scott believed in the protocol, but he wasn't taking any chances with a man who'd already proven himself to be a too-capable killer. If he could get a shot, he was taking it.

"I have no intent of hitting you now, either," Connors said, but he didn't move his weapon from where he held it against Chelsie's head. "I wasn't expecting such a crowd, but give me a few minutes of your time and then you can all go home."

"You want to explain why," Chelsie said, her tone softer than usual.

Apparently this was her negotiator voice. Scott had to admit, it was good. He'd never heard her in action.

"You didn't take the chance in the courtroom," Chelsie added before Connors could answer. "But that doesn't mean you can't now. Let us take you back and we'll find you a reporter. Whoever you want. We can make sure your side of the story comes out, so people understand."

Connors snorted. "I don't want to talk to some reporter, back in jail. And I could care less if people understand." His voice slowed. "No one's going to understand. There's nothing to understand. I was out of my mind. I deserve what I got."

He paused and Scott shifted his hands slightly. He was still gripping his Glock, but he needed a target.

Chelsie's conversation was working, at least to distract Connors from Scott, because as Scott inched a tiny bit farther left, Connors continued, "I want to talk to you, Chelsie. A year ago, you told me we could talk things through. Well, now I'm taking you up on that."

"Okay—"

"I don't want to hear your negotiator line." Connors cut Chelsie off. "Now pay attention. We don't have a lot of time."

"Sure we do," Ella said. "We have as much time as you need."

Connors straightened a little, showing himself over Chelsie's head for the first time as he glared at Ella. But his gun hand stayed steady. And he didn't raise up enough to give Scott the kill shot he needed—because if he wanted to eliminate Connors's motor functions instantly, the area he had to hit was very, very specific. And very, very small.

As a trained sharpshooter himself, Connors knew it, knew exactly how much of himself he could show. Scott wasn't sure why he was giving them even this much.

Maybe it was to send a message to Scott and Andre, telling them that he knew exactly what they were trying to do.

The man looked awful. Bloodshot eyes, gaunt features, exhaustion evident in the deep circles underneath his eyes. But as he studied the man, Scott realized that unlike the way he was during the trial, Connors wasn't on anything now.

That was both good and bad. Good because he was less likely to make an irrational decision without warning. Bad because he probably had full motor control. At the time of the massacre, he'd had a lot of painkillers in his system, but it hadn't prevented him from hitting every single target dead on. Completely sober, with his shooting skills, unless they got very, very lucky, Connors could probably take out both Chelsie and Ella before he or Andre could so much as raise their weapons.

"This wasn't my idea," Connors said unexpectedly and as he ducked back down behind Chelsie again, Scott realized he wasn't talking to them. He was only talking to Chelsie.

Ella's hands were slowly coming down and Connors jabbed his weapon at her long enough for her to lift them high over her head again. Then he pressed it back against Chelsie's skull.

"Whose idea was it?" Chelsie asked, but there was a hitch in her voice telling Scott she wasn't sure she was taking the right negotiation approach.

Scott moved again. A tiny slide of his right foot, then a tiny shift of his left one. He still didn't have an angle on Connors, but if Chelsie could keep him occupied...

"A friend," Connors said, but the way he spat the word, it was clear the friendship was over.

"A friend told you to come here that day?" Chelsie asked. "And it's not fair that he's free, no consequences?"

"That's not the point," Connors said, waving his gun around behind Chelsie's head.

He was agitated. A string of curses ran through Scott's mind as he moved again, slowly, too slowly.

"His name's Mike Danvers. He transferred out of our unit right before..." Connors paused. "Right before that IED blew. A few days before."

"Did he have something to do with the IED?"

Chelsie asked. "I'm pretty familiar with how the military works, Clayton. Did you know that? Did you know my parents were in the army? I can help you. Please lower the weapon so we can talk about this face to face."

"Danvers had nothing to do with the IED. Listen," Connors barked. The gun shifted, pointing past Chelsie directly at Scott, even as Connors kept his face hidden behind her. "Don't move!"

In that split second, Scott calculated the distance and the angles. He could fire at Connors's left leg, but it wouldn't hit an artery. And Connors was a soldier at heart. If he fired, would Chelsie move out of the way fast enough for Scott to take the kill shot, or would Connors still get her?

Scott's fingers twitched with the need to squeeze the trigger, because Connors was becoming more and more agitated. But he couldn't be sure, so he froze.

Then Connors put his gun back on Chelsie, and Scott's chance was over.

"Stop talking," Connors demanded. "Just listen."

Her head bobbed up and down and Scott's gaze took in Andre and Ella, both tense. He could see the weariness in Ella's face as she continued to hold her hands up above her head, something that would put a shake in her hand if she had the chance to go for her gun. He recognized the somber expression on Andre's face. Andre didn't think this was going to end well.

"I was brainwashed, okay?" Connors said. "I was already on painkillers, and they gave me more—a lot of them. They knew how pissed I was with the military—that IED, it shouldn't have happened. We never should have been on that road—we knew it was controlled by militants, and they never should have made us take that route. Honestly, they never should have sent our unit at all. We'd just come off another mission and we were all wiped out. If we'd been fresh, we'd have seen the signs. But they said there was no one else to go. So it was our unit. Again."

Connors's knuckles whitened around his weapon. "Then they sent the one guy—the *one guy*—who should have been there, in that armored truck with us. The only other person besides me who was meant to die that day, but didn't. And he's the one who pitched this to me."

Emotions flashed across Chelsie's face too fast for Scott to evaluate, and then she said softly, "Mike Danvers."

Scott assumed she'd said the name to prove to Connors she'd been listening to him, rule number one in negotiations.

It must have been the right move, because as Scott inched a little farther right, finally enough to get a glimpse of Connors behind Chelsie, Connors visibly relaxed.

"Yes. That's right. It was Mike who gave me the idea. He's the one who convinced me to do it." He nodded, his shoulders coming down, and for the first time since they'd arrived, Scott had hope for a peaceful ending.

"You want him to take his share of the blame for what happened," Chelsie said. "I understand that, Clayton. And it's got to be done the right way this time. You realize that, don't you? I can open an investigation."

"I know you're feeding me a line of BS here, Chelsie. The military has negotiators, too. But the thing is, I checked up on you. And you're going to look into this for me, because you won't be able to help yourself. Because you need your own answers about that day. Am I right?"

"Yes," Chelsie whispered. Then, louder, "How do I find Mike?"

"If I could answer that, I wouldn't need you. He's gone to ground. But this wasn't some plan he hatched on his own. He's not that smart, and he's not that bloodthirsty. Someone was using him to get to me. I want to find out who set me up for this. And I want to find out why."

"Why now, Clayton?" Chelsie asked, as Scott moved his weapon up, millimeter by millimeter, in case it all went wrong.

"I got clean," Connors replied, genuine pain in his voice. "And it finally hit me what I did, that my revenge was misplaced and—" He paused, then continued, "But I also realized there's an agenda here. There's a reason they wanted me to shoot those people. And it wasn't at all why Mike said I should do it. The people at the recruitment booth had nothing to do with the decision to send us on the mission that killed the rest of my team." His tone turned angry, and his gun hand shook a little. "Someone played me. And I'm not going down alone."

Ella's expression turned panicked at the same moment it occurred to Scott that this could be an endgame. Connors's plan could be to take out Chelsie, along with himself.

Scott drew a breath, ready to lift his weapon and squeeze the trigger on the exhale, when the crack of a gunshot split the air. And it wasn't Connors who'd fired.

"Move!" Scott screamed as Connors whipped his own weapon left, away from Chelsie and Ella, toward the new threat.

Chelsie grabbed Ella's arm and the two of them ran for the shelter of the community center, the same place Chelsie had crouched a year ago, thinking she was hidden from Connors's scope.

Andre raced toward Scott, keeping his gun steady on Connors the whole time, as Scott searched for the new shooter. Beyond the glow of the light above the parking lot, everything was dark.

There wasn't much around the community center. A lot of empty farmland that made a gunshot echo. Those bleachers. A few barns. Where was the shooter? Who was he trying to hit?

Scott ran backward as he searched for a target with his Glock, not an ideal option for a distance shot even if he could see anything. Andre was beside him, as Connors suddenly turned and raced away from the parking lot, toward the bleachers where he'd parked a year ago.

Was it where his partner waited now?

Another *boom* echoed, and the lightbulb above shattered, glass falling around them as the parking lot plunged into darkness.

Chapter Seven

"Move! Move! Move!"

Darkness surrounded her as Chelsie ran, bumping her way along the inside of the U-shaped enclosure outside the community center. The bricks abraded her right hand, and Ella's elbow was still clutched tight in her left one. The world had gone silent after the two gunshots, except for the ringing in her ears and the too-loud memory of the screams she'd heard here a year ago.

Somewhere behind her, Scott and Andre were still out in the open, still exposed.

Of course, if the shooter was high in the bleachers where Connors had been during his shooting spree, then so were she and Ella. Chelsie yanked Ella across to the other side of the enclosure, where a bullet fired from the bleachers couldn't hit them.

Her ears were still recovering from the gunshots, but she thought she heard boots racing toward her. Scott or Andre? Or Connors?

Chelsie spun, dropping Ella's arm, and ripped her weapon from its holster. She blinked, but her eyes were adjusting too slowly. Spots of light flashed over her eyeballs, the aftereffects of glancing back as the lightbulb shattered. A figure was coming closer. Or was it two?

"It's us, Chelsie," Scott said.

The tension in her chest loosened a fraction. He hadn't been hit.

"Keep moving," Andre whispered, and as Chelsie spun back for the community-center door, there was another loud boom.

Someone was still shooting.

"Go," Scott commanded. "The second guy isn't on the bleachers. He's out front. He could still hit us." He and Andre turned away from them, aiming their weapons into the darkness, blocking her and Ella from harm.

She didn't want either of them to die for her.

Things started to come into focus as Chelsie dragged her T-shirt down over her elbow and slammed it into the glass on the top half of the door. The impact sent pain ricocheting up to her shoulder, but the glass cracked and a second jab broke it. Yanking her elbow free, she stuck her hand through the opening and reached for the locked handle on the other side, the broken glass scraping up her arm. With a twist, the door was open and she wrenched her hand free, ignoring the stinging on her skin as she pulled the door wide and darted inside.

Ella followed fast behind her and then finally, finally, Scott and Andre were in the building, too.

"Come on," Scott said, moving out in front. "Let's get into an interior room and call for backup."

Three more gunshots drowned out his next words.

"Got it," Andre said, dialing his cell phone. "Shots fired," he reported "Four SAs on site. We've got two shooters, one active. The other is Clayton Connors."

"Is that a car?" Scott interrupted and Andre paused.

In the distance, Chelsie heard a car rev to life and burn rubber as it took off. She looked at Scott, as he continued to herd them all into a center room.

His expression was focused, the way it had been as she'd tried to talk Connors down, and she could see him trying to figure out exactly where the car had been parked.

"Near the bleachers," she whispered.

Then another car gunned it, this one from the direction where Scott had said the shooter was hiding.

"We suspect they're on the move now," Andre added, still on the phone, and then Chelsie stopped listening as Scott turned around to face her. He was glaring, his dark eyes narrowed into slits.

"What did you think you were doing? You could have gotten yourself—and Ella—killed!"

"Ella can take care of herself," Ella spoke up drily.

Scott turned his glare toward her. "From where I was standing, kiddo, you weren't doing a particularly good job of it."

"Stop," Chelsie said, moving so she was standing between Scott and Ella. "I called Ella. You want to throw blame around, fine. But it's not Ella's fault, so you can just lay it on *me*."

She expected him to do it, to yell at her about leaving protective custody to return to the scene of the crime and dragging one of his closest friends into danger. But he merely stared at her, his jaw locked so tight she could see the muscles clench.

Then Ella moved forward and patted him on the arm like only someone who was as close as family could do. "You need to excuse Scott. He takes the big brother role a little too seriously."

"Chelsie's *not* like a sister," he snapped.

Chelsie cringed at his tone, but Ella turned to face her. As her friend stared, Chelsie felt her skin flush from her neck to her ears.

Ella pressed her lips together, as if she was suppressing a smile. Finally, she nodded and turned back to Scott, who looked a little embarrassed himself.

"If you're finished with your little soap opera over here," Andre spoke up, "backup is on the way."

"Good," Scott said, instantly back to business, his expression serious. "The shooters are probably gone, but we'll stay right here until backup arrives."

Scott holstered his weapon, making Chelsie realize she was still clutching her own Glock too tightly. She did the same, cringing as she noticed the shard of glass in her forearm.

Suddenly, Scott was close again, and he was

back to scowling, but this time all his attention was on her arm. He carefully picked out a little piece of glass, and she barely felt it since his other hand was around hers, holding her arm up for better access.

Here she was, bleeding and hiding from a shooter, and all she could think of was his hand around hers. She eased her arm carefully free. It stung, but all it needed was a little hydrogen peroxide and she'd be fine. "Thanks."

With him so close to her, the rest of the room—the rest of the world—seemed to fade away. What was it about this guy that made her lose all sense?

She stepped back, forcing herself to ignore the way her body reacted to Scott's nearness, and corrected his statement that there'd been two shooters. "Connors wasn't actually shooting."

"Not this time," Scott said.

Ella moved beside Scott and looked at Chelsie. "You don't think the other shooter was firing at us, do you?"

Chelsie shook her head. "Those gunshots continued after we were all inside. I think he was shooting at Connors."

"I CAN'T BELIEVE you fell for Connors's garbage." Scott stared at her, his normally magnetic gaze harsh and unforgiving.

She'd thought he was going to hold his tongue. The whole drive back from the community center, he'd brooded silently in the passenger seat while she'd sat in back, waiting for the inevitable explosion. When it hadn't come, she'd thought she'd gotten lucky.

But the second they'd walked through the door of the safe house, he'd faced her, moving so close they were almost touching, blocking her way. He wasn't yelling, but his quiet anger was worse.

"If he was trying to kill me, he had the opportunity," she said, refusing to step away from him like she wanted to do.

"I'm going to let you two hash this out," Andre said, trying to walk past them.

But Chelsie wasn't letting him off the hook that easily, and she snagged his sleeve before he could leave the kitchen. "Connors could have fired on me before I even knew he was there. He wasn't trying to kill me."

Andre slowed to a stop and crossed his arms over his chest, frowning at both of them.

"Or it could be that he didn't kill you because he knew if he did, he had no bargaining chip," Scott said. "A hostage kept him alive. If he'd shot you and run, he wouldn't have made it three steps before I took him down."

"Why am I here again?" Andre asked quietly.

Ignoring him, Chelsie answered, "Okay, then why did the second shooter keep firing after we were all inside? He wasn't shooting at us. He was shooting at *Connors*."

"Or he wanted us to think that," Scott said. "If he was aiming at Connors, he's either a piss-poor shot or he missed on purpose. But he sure got that light dead on."

"Which gave Connors an exit strategy," Andre agreed. "The *only* exit strategy where he didn't end up dead or in handcuffs."

"Maybe the plan was to take us all out, but he couldn't do it and ensure Connors's safety, so he blew out the light instead," Scott added. "And then it was too dark for him to hit us."

A niggling doubt started inside her mind; their argument made a lot of sense. Except that she'd been 100 percent focused on Connors and the gun barrel against her skull. Her negotiator training dealt intensely with the small signals, like language choices, tone and volume of the voice. All the little things that would give clues to intent if she couldn't see the person she had to talk down—which was common for negotiators. And Connors's voice had held too much conviction.

"You don't believe *anything* he said?" Chelsie asked.

"Come on, Chelsie. How long have you been in the Bureau? Conspiracies are pretty rare because they don't work. Someone always blabs. Besides, what reason would this Danvers guy have to convince Connors to kill those people? Connors, on the other hand, had a pretty strong motive, all on his own."

"Still, someone kept shooting after we were inside—"

"He was trying to keep us inside," Scott interrupted.

"I don't think so. I don't think that guy was with Connors. Connors believed what he was telling us."

"He might believe it, but that doesn't make it true," Andre said. "He admitted he was drug addicted at the time of the shooting. He could've hallucinated Danvers's involvement. Or he convinced himself of it while he was in jail, because he couldn't handle the guilt."

It made sense, but somehow Chelsie knew

they were wrong. "There was something in his voice…"

"Did you talk to him a year ago?" Scott asked. "I'm aware that *you* talked, but did he? Did he say anything to you that day?"

She wished he had. She wished he'd given her anything—any opening to try to get through to him. Maybe if she'd had a more experienced negotiator with her, like Martin Jennings… But Martin hadn't made it on time. This was on her.

"You read the file. He didn't say anything. He just fired." And kept firing, until the only person left alive was her.

A familiar anguish welled up, the knowledge that it had been her job to save all those people and even though she'd failed them, she'd still gotten to walk away.

Scott must have seen the despair on her face. "When we fill out our report, someone will run down Danvers. If there's any truth to Connors's story, we'll find it. But otherwise, that means Connors has someone helping him."

He was right, but suddenly it wasn't good enough for Chelsie. Suddenly, she needed to go through the case file, like Scott had wanted her to do from the start. "If he only planned to show up and kill me, what did he need a long-distance shooter for? Besides, he could have killed me a year ago, right? And he didn't. So why do it now?"

Before Scott could theorize, she continued, "He knew I would be there, but he didn't know I'd have a couple of HRT snipers in tow. Why would he need help?"

"Insurance, Chelsie. You may not be a sniper, but you're still FBI. There's the possibility that the extra shooter was there *just* to make sure Connors could give his side of the story without being arrested, and he had no intention of killing you. But that's assuming this guy was helping Connors, *not* trying to kill him."

Chelsie stepped back, ready to go around Scott and find his laptop, start digging. "I still think those bullets were intended for Connors. The question is, why?"

Scott moved in front of her, blocking her way. The anger was back in his expression, but it was mingled with something else now, something that made her skin tingle. "You really think you're getting off that easy?"

She glanced around him for help from Andre, only to discover he'd somehow slipped out of the room without her noticing.

Refusing to let Scott see how much effect he had on her, she straightened her shoulders and said stiffly, "I apologize for sneaking off."

"And for stealing my SUV?" he demanded, some of his anger fading behind a grin.

She tried to keep from matching his smile. "That, too. If it makes you feel better, I was only planning to borrow it."

It was the wrong thing to say, because all amusement left Scott's face and he moved forward, until he was so close they were touching.

She leaned her head back so she could look

into his eyes, then realized that was a mistake. The anger on his face didn't begin to cover the desire underneath.

For a long moment, the whole room seemed to still as she waited for him to lean a little bit closer. To press his lips against hers and make her forget that she was hiding from a killer who seemed to want her help in proving he hadn't acted alone. To make her forget the failure that had led her to this moment, the memories of those men dying that never seemed to be far from her mind. To make her forget everything except how good they could be together, even if it was only for one more night.

But he didn't move. He just stared at her, as though he was waiting for her to lean in.

She couldn't do it. If she reached for him, whatever happened between them would be her fault. And she'd made too many mistakes a year ago, mistakes she'd promised herself she wouldn't repeat.

Suddenly realizing she'd literally been holding

her breath, Chelsie exhaled and said, "I think we should review the file again."

At the same time, Scott barked, "You could have gotten yourself killed tonight, Chelsie."

And then he did lean forward, but instead of the aggressive, all-consuming kiss she'd expected, he folded her carefully into his arms.

She sank into his embrace as though she belonged there, and closed her eyes. His arms felt strong and capable around her, and she felt his hand brush comfortingly over her hair.

With her face pressed against his neck, the scents of aftershave and sweat and cordite filled her nose, and she remembered he'd come for her at the WFO straight from another mission. She breathed deep, and the smell of him reminded her of being in his house.

When she thought about that day, she usually remembered the intensity of the sex, the rush she'd felt at being in his arms. Now, the little details came back, the way he'd held her hand under the bar as they'd talked at Shields, the ridiculous things he'd said to her as they'd rushed for his bedroom. Things about how his friends were going to be jealous he'd spotted her first, how he wanted to hear all about her new job, where he wanted to take her for their second date.

Nonsense they'd never gotten to because they'd quickly become too busy taking each other's clothes off. And then she'd refused all his efforts to go out with her again.

It never would have gone anywhere, not after the shooting for sure, and given his reputation, probably not even if it hadn't happened. And yet, being in his arms again now, it almost felt as if it could have.

She put her arms around his waist and held on, not wanting to move. The hug was platonic, almost familial, and yet, somehow it was the closest she'd ever felt to him. It was the kind of touch she'd share with a boyfriend, not a one-night stand.

Her muscles relaxed as the residual adrenaline seeped out of her. She tightened her hold on him as she thought about how he'd stayed out in the open while she and Ella ran for safety. He could have been killed tonight, and it would have been her fault.

Her fault. Again.

Pain spread outward from her chest and she squeezed her eyes more tightly closed. He was fine. Andre was fine. Ella was fine.

But when she thought about what could have happened, a sob welled up in her throat. She drew shallow breaths, trying to hold it in, but this close to her, there was no way Scott wouldn't feel her distress.

He brushed the hair back from her ear and she felt his breath there, and that fast, her pain faded underneath a new tension as she waited to feel the touch of his lips, his teeth, his tongue.

Instead, he whispered in her ear, "You couldn't have known Connors would be there." She shook her head, but he pressed on. "I didn't like you going somewhere without me right now, but neither of us expected to see Connors there. This isn't your fault."

"Ha," she snorted angrily. "It *was* my fault. Every time I go to that community center, I put people at—"

She cut herself off, but when she tried to push away from him, Scott held on tighter. "Don't do that to yourself. You know it isn't true."

She shoved again, harder this time, and broke free of his arms. She stumbled backward, bumping the wall, and then righted herself.

When he stepped toward her, she held up a hand that was embarrassingly shaky. "I'm just tired. I'm going to get some sleep. In the morning, I'll review that file with you. And I want to do a search on Mike Danvers, too."

She turned and fled for her bedroom before he could stop her again.

"DO I NEED to worry about her sneaking out the bedroom window?" Andre asked without looking up from his book as Scott walked into the living room and sank onto the couch.

He'd tried for half an hour to go to bed after talking to Chelsie, then given up. Scott sighed, even though he knew Andre was joking. The window in the back bedroom was painted shut; Chelsie wasn't getting out that way without making a ton of noise. He leaned his head back against the couch, knowing there was a good chance he'd be falling asleep here soon.

From the pointed glance Andre gave him, his partner knew it, too.

"She's not going anywhere. She's blaming herself for tonight."

"Well, she shouldn't have left without us," Andre said, "but none of us expected Connors to be there."

"Yeah, I tried to tell her—"

"Still, that's the whole point of protective custody." Andre shut his book. "We can't identify where the threat is or we wouldn't need to be in hiding, right? She's Bureau. She should know better."

Scott glanced down the darkened hallway, hoping Chelsie was sound asleep by now and couldn't hear them.

"You can't deny I'm right," Andre said. "But I understand it. If it was me that guy was coming after, I'd have a hard time hiding out and letting someone else handle it, too."

"She's blaming herself for all of it," Scott said, only half paying attention to Andre now as he leaned his head back again. "What happened a year ago. Tonight. I honestly don't get it. She was counterterror before she went into negotiation. It's not like she hasn't seen cases like this before."

"Well, it's different when you're the one who has to reason with an irrational, drug-addicted killer."

"Sure, but—"

"Seriously," Andre interrupted. "Think about it. We show up and we go in and take the guy down, whoever he is. What's the worst part about our job?"

"The waiting," Scott replied, not having to think about it.

"Right. And in a way, that's all she does. You've worked with enough negotiators. She has to sit there from a distance and deal with the targets on their timetables, sometimes pretending she agrees with what they say. And then, at the end of it, talking still might not work." Andre shuddered a little. "I'd *hate* that job."

"Yeah. But she picked the specialty."

"She was good with Connors today," Andre said. "For a while there, she was getting through to him."

"Until the end," Scott agreed. When the gunfire had started, he'd been sure Connors was planning a murder-suicide.

"Well, there's a reason negotiators never go to a scene by themselves."

When Scott didn't respond, Andre tapped

him on the leg with his book. "Go catch some sleep, man."

"Yeah, yeah." Scott pushed himself off the couch. Sleep *did* sound good. Not as good as—

A gasp and a curse from Chelsie's room cut off his thoughts, and Scott was suddenly wide-awake. Hand over his holster, he double-timed it to her door and opened it fast.

She turned to him. She was sitting upright in her bed as though she'd woken suddenly, but she was alone in the room. Of course she was. No one could have gotten in that way. He was overtired, which was why it was Andre's turn to be on watch.

His eyes adjusted quickly to the darkened room. He was about to apologize, but the words died on his lips as he stepped closer. She *did* look as if she'd been scared out of sleep. "What's wrong?"

"Nothing." She shook her head, obviously lying. "Nothing."

And then he realized. "Going to sleep right

after what happened probably wasn't the best idea."

She scowled at him, and even with her blond hair ratted up from sleep, and her eyes narrowed into slits, he couldn't help himself from moving closer, until he was standing beside her bed.

"I was dreaming about what happened a year ago. About what I said to Connors."

Scott sat down on the edge of the bed, and she shifted her legs away from him. "What did you say?"

She folded her knees into her chest. "Nothing that worked." She stared past him as she continued. "I tried the standard methods I learned in training. The first priority is to get the subject talking, to make a connection with him, establish trust. But we never got that far. It happened fast. And no matter what I did, he never said a word to me."

"But obviously you made an impression," Scott replied, turning so he was facing her more fully. "He let you live. And he chose *you* to help him. He does trust you. Why?"

Deeper creases formed between her eyebrows, and just when he thought she didn't know, she said, "If he *had* decided to shoot me that day—"

"Don't go down that road," Scott interrupted.

She put her hand on his arm, leaning closer. "Hear me out. If he had decided to shoot me, when would he have done it?"

Scott didn't like the question, but he suddenly knew why she was asking. "Well, his original targets were the military officers. He chose that spot for a reason, and he didn't wait for visitors to show up, which he could have done if he wanted a higher body count. So, I'd say—unless you said something that really pissed him off—he would have waited until he hit his primary targets and then taken you last."

She nodded, her eyes clear and wide-awake as they met his. "The last thing I said to him before it was too late to help anyone was that he wasn't alone."

Chapter Eight

"You think he views me as some kind of accomplice to what he did that day?" Chelsie asked, feeling sick.

As a negotiator, it was her job to try to analyze what the target was thinking, what they wanted, what would draw them out. It was a key rule in negotiations not to lie to a target unless absolutely necessary, but stretching the truth was pretty common. Because it was hard to form a connection with someone unless that person felt like you sympathized. And given the reasons a negotiator would be needed, it was always going to be tough to sympathize.

Sure, in training, she had learned to break down all the bad choices and bad luck and sometimes the bad things that had happened *to* the target to get them to this point. Understanding the subject was key. But taking that final step and sympathizing with a potential killer? She didn't need to do that. She just had to convince the perp she did.

In all of the practice scenarios she'd run with CNU, that part had been simple. Even the worst of them usually had some core need she could identify with—a man taking his own child hostage might do it because he hated his ex-wife, but usually it was because he loved his kid. And so she'd been trained to recognize and use that love to convince him he wasn't going to endear himself to his kid by taking the child away from Mom. Breaking it down like that was how Chelsie had been taught to approach a scene.

What did the target really need? Not his demands, but his needs. And how could she convince him she could help him get what he wanted?

Except with Connors, she'd had no idea what he'd wanted. So, she'd tried everything and nothing seemed to work. Until the end, when she'd told him he wasn't alone, that she was there to help him. There had been one military officer—the man with the one-year-old daughter—still alive, still running for her. And he'd almost made it. Connors had paused a tiny bit longer between shots that time. He'd still taken it, but then he'd stopped. He hadn't killed her.

She glanced at Scott and realized he'd been talking. "What?"

"Chelsie." Scott put his hand over hers, which was resting on his arm. She didn't even remember putting it there.

"He didn't have any close family, right?" she asked.

"Connors? No, his file said—"

"We should see if anyone visited him in jail."

"Okay, but come on, Chelsie, you can't honestly—"

She smiled at him. It was a pathetic excuse for a smile, she could tell, but he looked so worried about her. "I know. It's not my fault."

"Do you know?" Scott leaned closer. "Because it sure seems like you've been carrying this around with you for a year."

She had. The guilt was always there. And now that Connors was out of jail, asking for her help, there was no way to hide from it anymore. And if she could start working through the consequences of that day, maybe it was time to stop hiding from what had happened with Scott, too.

Maybe it was time to stop denying that although that night had mostly been about sex, she had genuine feelings for this man. What exactly those feelings were was the hard part. But the thought of him with someone else filled her with jealousy. And the way he was staring at her now, with so much concern and caring, made need rise up inside her. A need to feel his arms around her again, to feel his lips on hers, to be able to rest her hand on his arm in public like Ella had done at the community center. To have a relationship with him that went beyond the bedroom.

Surprise flashed across his face as she leaned toward him.

He slid his hand off hers, gliding it up her arm, and leaving goose bumps behind, until he hooked his arm around her back. His other hand slid underneath her, and suddenly she wasn't only leaning toward him, but being lifted onto his lap. Then his lips were caressing hers as his tongue slipped into her mouth.

She held on tighter, kissing him as though it had been years since she'd felt his mouth against hers, instead of only a few hours. Desire flamed fast, the way it had the first time with Scott, the way it had never done with anyone else.

Being close to him felt so strangely right, even

though she didn't really know enough about him for it to be anything but wrong. But at this moment she didn't care whether it was right or wrong. She only cared about being closer to him. She squirmed, trying to press herself against him, trying to peel his shirt off at the same time.

He smiled against her lips, pulled away from her just slightly to whisper, "Door's open."

His words made her freeze. If she did this, would rumors spread like they had in LA? Would she get a reputation at the Bureau as someone who slept around with other agents? Right now, so close to Scott, she couldn't bring herself to care as much as she knew she should.

"Close it," she demanded, getting a grip on the bottom of his shirt. She started to take it off, then got distracted by the muscles in his abdomen, and flattened her hands against his stomach instead.

He groaned into her mouth, and his hands started to roam over her back, his fingertips sliding down to her waist. He shifted her, fitting her against him better.

She wrapped her legs around his waist, wanting to make it easy for him to stand and carry her over to the door, kick it shut. She willed him to do it, not wanting to move her lips off his long enough to voice it. She shouldn't need to. He had to understand exactly what she wanted from the way she was rocking her hips against him.

"Ahh," he mumbled into her mouth. His fingers dug into her waist, stopping her, and then he was pushing her away. "Chelsie."

He shook his head, but his expression was a mixture of desire and desperation. If she slid back toward him, kept kissing him, it wouldn't take much convincing.

"Chelsie," he said again, his voice deeper than usual. "You're just upset about—" He gave a heavy sigh, as if he couldn't believe he was turning her down, then added, "I don't want a repeat of last time, where you wake up and sneak out on me."

Insulted, she moved the rest of the way off his lap. "Like you've never done that." He was the one who was practiced at one-night stands, not her. He should know how it worked.

"No," he said, his tone suddenly flat. "I haven't."

"Oh, come on—"

"No," he interrupted, standing up, looking pissed. "Yeah, I've had one-night stands. I'll admit it. But I've never done anything as cowardly as sneaking out on someone in the middle of the night."

Chelsie stood, fists on her hips, even though she knew it made her seem defensive. But her angry words died on her lips. How could she argue? She *was* a coward.

Or at least she'd been acting like a coward for the past year, running away from what had happened, instead of dealing with it head-on the way she knew she should.

It was time to start making a change. She squared her shoulders and dropped her hands to her sides. "You're right."

From his surprised expression, he'd expected an argument, but she rushed on before he could speak. "I shouldn't have done that. I was trying to avoid an awkward goodbye in the morning. Guess it was awkward either way."

It still was. Because as much as she wanted him—as much as part of her wanted a real chance with him—the truth was, she'd never be able to look at him and not see that community-center parking lot, bathed in blood.

"I think we need to try to forget about what happened between us last year, and focus on figuring out this case," she said. "Can you help me do that?"

He stared back at her, his expression unreadable, for so long that Chelsie started to fidget.

Finally, he nodded. "If that's what you want," he said, then stood staring at her as if he was waiting for more.

But what else was there to say? So, she simply nodded, and then Scott turned and walked out of her room, shutting the door quietly behind him.

"LONG NIGHT?" ANDRE greeted Scott the next morning with raised eyebrows.

Scott gratefully accepted the cup of coffee Andre held out to him, and drank. It was black, extra strong, the way Andre always made it. Usually Scott insisted on making his own when they were stuck on a job somewhere, but this morning he didn't mind. "Uh-huh," he muttered as the coffee burned its way down the back of his throat, clearing his mind.

Normally, long days bracketed by a few hours' sleep—sometimes outside on the ground in freezing cold weather—were no big deal to Scott. He'd had plenty of them in his year and a half at HRT. But he was usually great at blocking everything from his mind and falling instantly into a combat nap.

Not last night. Last night, he'd been plagued by nightmares of Connors holding that gun to Chelsie's head, of the dead men in body bags in that same parking lot. And then nightmares involving his sister Maggie had intruded, too.

He shuddered and Andre narrowed his eyes. "You okay?"

"Yeah. You can catch some sleep. I'm going to call my sister while Chelsie's still out cold." At least he assumed she was still sleeping. She hadn't come out of her room yet, and he knew she hadn't sneaked past Andre again.

Andre looked at Scott, understanding, and clapped a hand on Scott's arm, nearly making him spill his coffee. "Maggie doing okay?"

Andre hadn't heard what had happened with Maggie recently, but he was aware of her history. And like the rest of the country, he knew about the anniversary.

Every September 1, the Fishhook Rapist surfaced, abducting, raping and branding a young woman on the back of her neck with a hook.

Then he let her go, drugged and too disoriented to give a useful description, with all forensic evidence carefully erased, before he disappeared for another year. Despite the Bureau's best efforts, the snake had been free for coming up on a decade. And his first victim had been Scott's little sister.

Andre knew that Scott never, ever worked on September 1. He and Ella and Maggie always closed ranks and tried to distract themselves, hoping that year would be different, and leaning on each other when it wasn't. What Andre didn't know—what even their parents and their youngest sister, Nikki, didn't know—was that in the past six months, the Fishhook Rapist had started sending Maggie letters.

The anniversary was three months away, but because of those letters, if it had been anyone but Chelsie in trouble, Scott wouldn't have volunteered for the job.

Realizing Andre was staring at him, Scott said, "You know Maggie."

His sister was tough. She'd been twenty-one when that SOB had hurt her, but instead of letting it destroy her, she'd decided to join the FBI and stop guys like him from hurting others. He, Ella and Maggie had always been best friends, so the minute she'd announced her intentions, Scott and Ella had looked at each other and nodded, then told Maggie, "We're in."

He couldn't imagine what his life would have been like if they hadn't made that pact. He'd graduated from college a year before Maggie, and he'd been getting settled in his first job in PR. His life had seemed simple and easy, if not exactly fulfilling.

Now, HRT and the FBI felt as if it had always been his calling.

"She's strong," Andre agreed, bringing Scott out of his memories. "If she needs anything, obviously I'm there."

Scott nodded. "Thanks." If there was anyone outside of Ella he would have trusted to have Maggie's back, it was Andre. They'd only been partners for a year and a half, but HRT was a brotherhood. And he'd gotten partnered with the most loyal guy on the team.

"Ella doing okay?"

"Yeah, she's fine. I tried to talk her into staying with us here, but she insists Connors was only using her to get to Chelsie, and I can't argue with that. There's no reason for him to go after Ella. And her fiancé may not be FBI, but he's probably going to smother Ella by watching out for her worse than I would. I did talk them into staying somewhere else until Connors is caught."

"Good," Andre said. "Well, I'm gonna catch some Zs." He walked down the hall, calling after him, "If you pick up where you left off last night, close the door this time, okay?"

Scott cursed, calling Andre some of the most creative names he could come up with, which just made his partner laugh. As Andre disappeared into his room, Scott picked up his cell phone. Time to check on Maggie.

Fear and anger mingled together, like they always did when he thought about his sister's rapist. He'd always thought Maggie was safe at school, even after he graduated and couldn't watch over her. She was smart, she was strong. And yet, one awful night had changed her life forever. And he hadn't been able to do anything about it. Even now, almost ten years later, he felt just as helpless when it came to making sure Maggie was safe.

Which was stupid. She was an FBI SWAT agent. She could take care of herself. And if he ever found the Fishhook Rapist, Scott could take him out from nearly a mile away. The problem was, they'd never seen the guy. But he'd somehow figured out where Maggie lived, figured out a way to torture her all over again with his sick letters.

As the phone rang, Scott gulped down his last mouthful of the sludge Andre tried to pass off as coffee.

"Hey, Scott. How's the job going?" his sister answered, her tone cheery. Too cheery.

"What happened?" he demanded.

"Nothing," she replied, sounding exasperated. "Long day is all."

Scott looked at his watch. "It's seven o'clock"

"Yeah, well, we handled a high-risk raid last night. I got home about an hour ago."

He heard something thump in the background, and then the same sound again, and realized she was kicking off the combat-style boots she liked to wear, even in eighty-degree weather. "Well, I won't keep you up much longer. I just wanted to check in."

Behind him, Scott heard light footsteps, and he straightened, glancing back. Chelsie stood barefoot in the hallway, as though she wasn't sure if she should turn around and go back to her room.

He gestured her forward with his hand, then turned away again. "Everything the same?" he asked Maggie. She'd understand that what he meant was, *No more contact from the Fish-hook Rapist?*

"Nothing new," she replied, weariness and anger in her voice. The way she sounded every time this topic came up. "It's been a month now since he's made contact. I think—"

"What?" Scott demanded when she cut herself off.

"Never mind. It's nothing urgent. We'll talk about it when you finish your detail. How's that going, by the way?"

Scott looked over his shoulder as Chelsie came timidly into the room and poured herself a cup of coffee. "I wouldn't drink that without a lot of cream," he warned her.

"What?" Maggie asked.

"Nothing. I'll check in tomorrow, okay? Call if you need me."

"I'll be fine. You don't need to worry so much. This jerk researched me enough to figure out where to send the letters, which means he knows what I do for a living. Which is why letters are all he'll dare to do." Pride tinged her voice when she asked, "I mean, do you want to go up against me?"

"Not a chance," Scott replied immediately. In HRT, he spent a lot more time than Maggie did on tactical training, because his role was full-time. Hers wasn't—it was on top of a regular special agent position. But Maggie's SWAT team had trained with a group from HRT once, and his sister had done him proud. She'd taken two of his teammates down using their own methods—speed, surprise and violence of action.

Still, no matter how strong and resourceful she was, no matter how much training she had, she was always going to be his little sister. And he was never going to stop worrying or wanting to protect her.

"I'll call you later," Maggie said.

"You better. Talk to you tomorrow."

Scott ended the call and glanced over at Chelsie, who was studiously avoiding his gaze as she sipped her coffee, cringing.

"I told you to add cream," Scott said. "That was Maggie," he added, and the relief on her face verified that his suspicion had been right. She'd thought he was talking to a girlfriend.

He stood and walked over to her, leaning against the counter as he studied her face. "You really think I'd kiss you if I was seeing someone?"

She looked away, then frowned as if she was thinking about it. "I guess not," she finally replied.

"Thanks for the vote of confidence." He stepped away from the counter and walked toward the living room, where he'd left his laptop. What kind of jerk did she think he was?

Sure, he'd had a lot of flings, both before he'd met her and after he'd realized she was never going to go out with him again. But he didn't date multiple women at once.

She trailed behind him. "Sorry. Yesterday,

on the phone, it sounded like—" She stopped, probably realizing she'd just told him she'd been eavesdropping.

"That was Maggie, too."

"It's not my business," she answered quickly.

"Well, I'm telling you anyway," he said, pissed at her and pissed at Connors and the whole situation. Pissed at himself, too. But if she insisted on viewing him as nothing more than an easy distraction, why was he trying for more?

Her hand on his arm stopped him. The simple touch made him want to spin around and take whatever she was offering.

"Is Maggie okay?" There was genuine worry in her voice.

Scott turned to face her, carefully pulling his arm free. Maggie and Chelsie were friends, but he doubted Maggie had shared what was happening. "She's fine."

Chelsie squinted at him, as if she knew he was lying. "Scott, if she needs you—"

"She's fine, Chelsie. Really."

"Okay," she said slowly, and he suspected she still didn't believe him. "Well, if you do need to go, you can. I'll be fine with Andre."

Scott held in a scowl. It sounded as though she'd prefer it if he were gone. "Protection is a two-man job. Minimum." He sat down and grabbed his laptop. "You're stuck with me."

"That's not what—" She shook her head and sat gingerly next to him, close enough to see his screen and far enough that they wouldn't be touching.

"All right," Scott said, waiting for his computer to boot up. "Let's find this Mike Danvers."

"I said I'd be fine because I thought about it some more last night," Chelsie burst out. "And I don't think Connors is after me. I honestly don't think I'm in any danger."

Annoyance filled him. The man had held a gun against her head mere hours ago and she thought she wasn't in any danger? "I don't care what you think," he snapped. "The FBI decided you're at risk, which means you're in protective custody."

He leveled a stare on her that he used in the field with targets who thought taking on an armed HRT agent in close quarters was a good idea. "You even think of leaving here again without me or Andre, and I'm cuffing you to the bed."

Instead of appearing intimidated, Chelsie raised one eyebrow. "Are you hitting on me again?"

"What?" Realizing what he'd said, Scott scowled back at her. "No, I'm not hitting on you. I'm trying to keep you from getting yourself killed, Chelsie! Don't be a fool." He leaned in close. "You think Connors was just trying to get your attention by threatening to blow your brains out all over that parking lot?"

His voice was gaining volume with every word, but he couldn't help himself. She wasn't taking the threat seriously enough. And no way was she putting herself in jeopardy again on his watch.

He couldn't deal with having another woman he cared about in danger.

Chelsie paled, her eyes wide and only inches away, and Scott kept going. "You remember what that parking lot looked like a year ago, right? You want to end up like that?"

"Of course I remember! I live with that image every single day!" She got loud, too, and suddenly she was in *his* face, and giving him the kind of stare that had probably made suspected terrorists back down during her counterterror days. "You're the one who said I needed to get inside his head. Well, guess what? That's what I did last night! And I believe him. I believe there's more to this."

She stared at him furiously, looking way too sexy with that scowl on her face.

Man, he loved when she was fired up. This was the woman he'd fallen for a year ago in

Shields, the woman who didn't let anyone or anything intimidate her.

"I'm going to find out what is going on here," she continued. "With or without your help."

Snatching his laptop off the couch, she strode into the kitchen with it, and all he could think as he watched her go was that he was in serious trouble. If the FBI didn't get Connors into custody soon, he was either going to lose his mind or his heart. And he wasn't really sure which would be worse.

Chapter Nine

"I can't believe they haven't found him yet," Andre muttered as he did push-ups on the floor in front of the living room couch.

"The military trained him to evade the enemy," Scott answered, not taking his gaze off the computer he had propped on his lap.

"Yeah," Andre snorted, not even breathing hard as he worked out. "Except we're not supposed to be the enemy."

It had been four days since Chelsie had sneaked out of the safe house. Since then, the FBI had investigated the shooting and put in a surveillance camera at the community center in case

Connors went back there for some reason. They had a nationwide BOLO out on the guy, and although plenty of tips had come in, Connors hadn't.

Despite his and Chelsie's best efforts, neither had Mike Danvers.

They'd verified Connors's claim that he and Danvers had served together, and that Danvers had transferred to another unit only a few days before the IED that killed everyone in his old unit except Connors. That incident had marked the end of Connors's military career. But Danvers had stayed in another six months before returning stateside.

Danvers had returned to his old house, now alone, since his wife had divorced him while he was overseas. He'd gone through a series of short-term jobs with defense contractors, all aboveboard as far as Scott could tell. Unlike Connors, the extent of Danvers's interaction with the law was two parking tickets.

Scott might have given up on Danvers as a

dead end right there except that he'd put in a call to the team handling Connors's escape and asked them to pay Danvers a visit. They'd tried. Repeatedly. But Connors had been right about one thing. Danvers wasn't where he should have been.

Danvers's phone was out of service, his house closed up and collecting newspapers on the stoop, and his ex-wife hadn't been able to find him in a few weeks, which she'd told the agents was unusual, since they shared custody of their daughter. Danvers had missed his last visit with her, and his ex-wife said he'd never skipped one when he wasn't overseas. She'd been worried, but she and Danvers weren't on the best of terms, so she hadn't pushed it and she hadn't filed a missing persons report. Her theory was that he'd been avoiding her because he'd met someone.

But the case agents thought more was going on, so they'd tried to track him through his work. Except that Danvers's last contract position working security analysis for a private firm had ended a month earlier and he hadn't gotten a new job. He was estranged from his family, but his friends weren't sure where he was, either. Like his ex-wife, they didn't seem particularly concerned—apparently Danvers wasn't the type to make regular plans with anyone. But no one seemed to think he'd taken a vacation. They'd all been surprised to learn he wasn't at home.

So where was he?

Had Danvers gone underground because he'd helped Connors escape? Or was he in hiding because Chelsie was right and he *had* tried to set Connors up to kill those people and now he thought Connors was after him? If that was the case, though, what was *his* motive to kill nine people he didn't know?

"I don't understand it," Scott said aloud, rubbing his eyes and giving up on the search he'd been running on Danvers for the past hour.

"Danvers?" Andre asked, flipping onto his back and starting a set of sit-ups.

Like Scott, Andre didn't like to sit still. Often, when they were called to a situation where a tactical solution might be needed, they found themselves on-site—sometimes for days or even months—while they waited for the green light. They'd learned to handle the waiting, but most HRT agents preferred action. When they weren't on assignment, they were either training, doing things like helicopter rappelling and target practice, or they were on call. Strenuous workouts were part of their job on a daily basis. Being stuck inside the safe house made it hard to do much.

"Yeah, Danvers," Scott replied, trying to ignore his own desire to do some pull-ups on the doorframe—or *something* to get his blood going. "If he's not involved in some way, that's pretty coincidental timing for him to disappear."

"Well, right or wrong, Connors obviously blames him. Maybe he killed Danvers."

"No. The investigators said it looked like Danvers hadn't been home in weeks. Since before Connors escaped."

"Well, he could be hiding from Connors. Same problem, I know. But what if he was involved in some way and felt guilty that only Connors was caught? He could have planned to help Connors escape, then realized Connors blamed him, and split from him."

Andre stopped his sit-ups, stretching his legs in front of him. "I've been thinking about what Chelsie said about the gunfire continuing after we were inside and I think she could be right about the second shooter aiming at Connors."

"Really? But—"

"There were gunshots well after we were inside. We weren't coming out again. By that point, the shooter should have been focusing on getting out of the area. He had to realize backup would be on the way. But he wasn't leaving. He was still shooting."

"I told you!" Chelsie said, appearing in the doorway.

Scott blinked at her, trying not to stare. She was wearing yoga pants and a tank top, her feet bare and her hair still wet from the shower. Droplets of water slid off her hair and down her arm.

They'd been tiptoeing around each other since he'd lost his temper with her a few days earlier, trying to treat each other like colleagues instead of former lovers. And he, at least, was failing miserably. Every time he saw her, he wanted to pick right back up where they'd left off.

Scott frowned at Andre and his partner shrugged. "What? I think it's possible. Is it the only possibility? No. But Chelsie's right. He could have been aiming at Connors."

Andre stood, stretching his arms over his head, and Chelsie's gaze went to his biceps, making Scott scowl.

"Okay. Let's say Danvers convinced Connors to shoot those people at the community center. You have any thoughts on Danvers's motive?" Scott asked Chelsie. "You went through the same information on Danvers's life that I did. This guy seems pretty normal. Having a little trouble readjusting to civilian life perhaps, but nothing like Connors. He's stable enough to hold down jobs, and his ex-wife may not like him, but she still trusts him, because she lets him take their daughter every other weekend."

"At the end of the day," Andre said, "Connors still dragged his rifle up those bleachers and murdered people. Even if Danvers suggested it, Connors only implied that he was too drugged up not to recognize it was a bad idea. He never said that Danvers was holding anything over him. It's not like Connors is going to get any leniency because someone else thought up the idea. He's the one who acted on it."

"I never said he wasn't culpable," Chelsie said, perching on the arm of the couch close to Scott.

Scott leaned slightly away. Chelsie didn't

seem to notice, but Andre gave him a questioning glance.

Ignoring his partner, Scott asked, "What motive would Danvers have had to convince Connors to shoot those people? Sure, Connors holds a grudge against the military. But Danvers doesn't. He just didn't re-up, probably because he could make better money in the private sector. Half his contracts were with a private security firm that works alongside the military."

Andre rolled his eyes. Scott knew his partner's feelings on security firms going overseas and taking jobs traditionally reserved for the military. Sometimes it was fine, and other times, employees not bound by the same rules as soldiers crossed lines that caused problems for everyone.

Chelsie frowned. "I honestly don't know. Unless he wanted one particular person out of the picture and he had Connors kill a group of them to make it seem random?"

Scott nodded thoughtfully. "That's certainly

happened before. We should take a closer look at each of the victims. I didn't see any obvious links between Danvers and the location or the victims when I checked yesterday, but I only did a cursory search."

"Great." Chelsie slid off the arm of the couch and onto the seat, close enough that her arm brushed his. Either she didn't notice or she didn't care. "Let's get started."

Scott moved his computer onto her lap and stood. "You can start. My eyes need a break."

"You're on watch," Andre reminded him. "I'm going to see if the treadmill in that back room works. You mind, Chelsie?"

Chelsie shook her head, already typing away. "Sure. Ignore the bra drying in the bathroom."

Andre was right. It was Scott's turn to keep watch. The area was difficult to sneak up on, even for a good marksman, and although he was pretty sure Chelsie wouldn't dare run off again on her own—and he and Andre had both hidden their keys—he liked her in someone's line of vision.

"Sure," Andre said, sounding completely uninterested in Chelsie's underwear—which was the only response good for his health.

Once Andre had left the room, Chelsie looked up at Scott. "Are you mad at me?"

Ever since he'd implied she was a coward a few nights ago, which he hadn't really meant, she'd started acting like the woman he remembered from Shields.

If he'd known that was all it would take to snap her out of the funk she'd been in for the past year, he would have done it a long time ago. But it was making him nervous. Downtrodden, passive Chelsie he had a chance at resisting. But take-charge Chelsie was exactly the woman he'd fallen for.

So, he'd been trying to keep what distance he could from her. And it bothered him that as soon as she'd snapped back to normal, she'd suddenly had no problem resisting *him*.

"No, I'm not mad," Scott answered as she stared at him expectantly.

"Okay," she replied, returning her attention to the computer. "How's Maggie doing?"

"She's fine."

Chelsie rolled her eyes. "I'm making an effort here. Can't you meet me halfway?"

What was that supposed to mean? He frowned, but answered, "How are your brothers?"

She seemed surprised, which was exactly how he felt. He hadn't expected to ask that, but now he realized he wanted to know. He wanted to know about her life. He wanted to know her, beyond the talented Special Agent, beyond the killer body, beyond the outer attitude and the inner vulnerability.

"I—" Her fingers went still on the keyboard. "I told you I had brothers?"

"No, you didn't. You told Andre."

"Oh. Right. Well, they're good. They're all on the other side of the country, so I don't see them often, but they do a lot together. Triplets," she added.

"Are you close to them?" Scott asked, settling back on the couch next to her.

Her gaze darted over to his, then back to the computer, and that fast, he realized something. She hadn't suddenly stopped being attracted to him. She'd just figured out how to hide it better.

"Uh, yeah," she said. "They're five years younger, so we didn't do a lot together growing up, but we're closer now. But you know, my parents are in Oregon and my brothers are in California, which is relatively close, and I'm way over here, so…"

"So you don't talk as much?"

"Not really."

"They don't like your job?" he guessed, knowing exactly what it was like to worry about family all the time.

"Well, they'd rather I'd stayed in advertising. They were shocked when I applied for the FBI, even though they knew I'd been thinking about it. I was the little princess, you know, and since— Well, they got over it. They're supportive."

"You always wanted to be FBI?"

"Well, not exactly. The military interested me, but my parents really pushed me to go for a safe career. So I ended up in advertising, but I couldn't tame that itch for more, and finally I decided to try for the FBI."

Scott leaned forward, trying to see her face as she bent over the laptop. His questions were making her uncomfortable, he could tell by the way her words sped up. Was it only because she didn't want to share anything personal with him or was there something specific she didn't want him to know?

Before he could figure out the best way to dig deeper, she broke in, "What about you?"

"What about me, what?"

"You're close to your family, right? I mean, you and Maggie are close, I know. What about everyone else?"

He nodded, but she had her eyes locked on the computer screen, despite having stopped typing a while ago. The questions felt like first-date getting-to-know-you stuff, the kind of things they should have asked each other a year ago. Except that on a first date, the woman probably would have given him some eye contact as she asked about his life.

"We're all pretty close. Maggie and I are only a year apart, so we were best friends growing up. Nikki's younger—she just graduated from college." Nikki making it safely through her college years had been a huge relief. She'd stayed home and commuted to school instead of living in the dorms like he and Maggie had. And he and Maggie had both gone over defensive techniques with Nikki until she'd sat them both down and insisted it was enough, that she'd be fine. And, thank goodness, she had been.

Chelsie looked over at him, finally. "I didn't know you had another sister."

"Yep. Nikki's the baby. My parents won't admit it, but she was pretty much their midlife crisis."

Chelsie fiddled with the locket around her neck, as though she was trying to come up with another question, and he reached out and turned the locket toward him. His fingers brushed hers, and she flinched at the contact and turned red.

He smiled at her, the kind of slow smile that had worked on her back in Shields, then looked at the worn gold heart locket, warm from her skin. "You always wear this."

It wasn't a question, but she nodded, reaching up and taking it from his hand, then turning away from him a little, her serious face on. "Yes. It was my mom's."

"Did she give it to you when you moved to DC?"

"No." Chelsie glanced down at the locket, running her fingers over it the way she always did when she was upset or nervous. "No, my dad remarried. My mom—really, she's my stepmom—is the one who lives in Oregon. She raised me, but my real mom died when I was a year old. This locket was hers. My dad gave it to me when I turned thirteen and I'm not sure I've ever taken it off since."

"I'm so sorry," he said, reaching for her hand.

She let him take her hand in his, let him brush his fingers over her palm. "I don't remember her. My stepmom and I are really close. But my mom's death—it's why my dad has a hard time with me being FBI. He supports me, don't get me wrong, but he and my mom were in the military. He left because she was killed on a tour of duty."

Suddenly everything snapped into place for Scott. Why this case had hit Chelsie so hard. Why she'd allowed it to destroy her career as a negotiator. Why it had made her question her ability to do the job at all.

She kept talking, about how her dad had started his own business, met and married her stepmom, and how she'd soon had three half brothers. But all he could think about was the debriefing after the shooting last year. The way she'd gone on and on about the man who'd died last that day, how he'd been one of the men determined to run to her side even as she tried to gesture for him to stay where he was. How he'd been talking to her as she'd tried to talk down Connors. How he'd cried about his year-old daughter and wanting to see her grow up, then run for her and gotten shot in the head.

Had she connected it yet? He stared back at her, seeing the vulnerability in her eyes as she talked about her past.

He took a breath, unsure how he was going to broach it, when Andre shouted from the other room.

"Scott! Chelsie! Get in here!"

Scott sprang to his feet, his hand automatically tightening around Chelsie's as he hauled her up with him. His laptop dropped to the floor and she started to reach for it, but he pulled her along with him, his free hand automatically resting over his Glock.

"What is it?" Scott demanded as he raced into the back bedroom, still clutching Chelsie's hand, keeping her slightly behind him.

Andre was standing on the treadmill, but he'd turned it off. He pointed at the ancient radio, and then turned up the volume.

"...escaped from prison five days ago," the radio announcer was saying. "Clayton Connors's mass shooting a year ago brought a new focus to the problem of PTSD and troops returning for too many tours in a row."

Chelsie took her hand out of his and stepped into the room, putting a little space between them, her focus entirely on the radio.

"This is a tragic way to get the public's attention," a new voice said. "But Connors is a prime example of what happens when a decorated soldier gets overworked, sees something traumatic and doesn't receive the help he needs. I think there could be a lot of other Connors out there, guys who keep being sent back overseas because they're needed and we don't have enough troops. The McCord-Siler bill was dead in the water before last year, but the Connors shooting put new life into it. I think it's finally going to pass."

"It's about time," the first voice agreed, and Andre lowered the volume.

"The bill is going to allow a lot more privatization of military security overseas. Right now, the military won't contract out some of that stuff, but once this bill passes, we're going to see a ton more of those private military security forces," Andre said. "There's a *lot* of money at stake here."

"And a lot of opportunities for ex-soldiers searching for a lucrative new career," Scott said. "Like Danvers."

Chapter Ten

"Is that a strong enough motive?" Chelsie asked, sitting cross-legged on the chair in the living room. The words from the radio ran through her mind over and over, but they seemed a long way from the events at the small rural community center in Virginia where the lives of nine people had been snuffed out.

Connors and Danvers were supposedly friends. Would Danvers really have convinced Connors to destroy his life—*and to kill people*—just to get a new job?

Andre and Scott stared back at her from the couch. Andre was still in workout clothes, but he'd barely broken a sweat. Scott wore low-slung jeans and a T-shirt, his hair neatly groomed but his face unshaven. Every time she looked at him, she imagined the feel of his scruffy jaw scratching against her chin, her neck, her chest.

Heat crept up her face as she stared at him, and she cursed her Irish heritage. If she blushed even a tiny bit, it showed on her cheeks like sunburn.

Scott's mouth curled knowingly, but all he said was, "Money usually is."

"Does he have any connection to this McCord-Siler bill? It seems like a pretty big stretch that Danvers would convince an old friend to kill a bunch of people he'd never met on the off-chance it would revitalize this bill and then get him hired."

"When you put it like that—" Andre started.

"Unless there was some reason for him to think the bill needed a poster boy," Scott interrupted. "Remember the notes from the case agents who talked to Danvers's wife? She said that after he left the military, she thought they'd be able to make a new start, but he'd basically been trying to do the same job for more money and with fewer rules."

"Still, he was working in military security before the shooting," Chelsie said. "And I'm not sure Connors makes a good poster boy."

"He's a poster boy for what the bill's founders always claimed they were trying to prevent," Andre said. "Exhausted troops overworked because there simply aren't enough of them. And then they snap. Connors is a pretty good example of what we don't want."

"You think the senators could be involved? McCord and Siler?" Chelsie was skeptical. Even though she'd been the first one to buy into Connors's claim someone had put him up to the shooting, Scott was right about conspiracies. The more people who knew about a plan like this, the more likely it was to blow up on them.

"Probably not," Andre said. "That's a huge risk of career-destroying jail time. Both of those guys have been around too long to be that stupid. McCord needs to boost his ratings if he's going to have any hope of reelection, but this is a stretch." He shook his head. "But Danvers might have heard the argument somewhere and decided to put it into action himself. I can't imagine a senator approaching Danvers and pitching a plan like this. But I *can* imagine someone like Danvers overhearing the idea and making it his own. He worked for Blackgate, right?"

Scott nodded. "Yeah, it was his most recent contract position."

"They're probably the firm that stands to gain the most if this bill passes." Andre leaned forward, deep lines appearing on his forehead. "Blackgate is huge. They've worked alongside the military for a few years now, but it's a reluctant partnership on the military's part. If this bill passes, though..."

"We're talking millions of dollars' worth of contract work, easy," Scott said. "Maybe someone at Blackgate was pulling Danvers's—or Connors's—strings?"

Andre nodded and Chelsie glanced back and forth between them. She knew a lot less about this, but HRT did work a lot with the military. Only last month, a unit from HRT had gone overseas and Chelsie had prayed Scott wouldn't be among them. She'd fumbled her way through asking Maggie about it, but her friend had been so distracted she hadn't noticed.

The thought made Chelsie frown. At the time, she'd just been relieved Maggie hadn't guessed Chelsie had feelings for her brother. But thinking back, she realized something had been wrong.

She glanced at Scott, wondering what all his check-in calls to Maggie were about. Had she been so busy burying herself in her own self-pity that she'd missed seeing her friend was in some kind of trouble?

"What?" Scott asked.

She shook her head. "What do you mean, what?"

He smiled at her, obviously amused. "You're scowling."

"Oh. Sorry." Instead of telling him what she'd really been wondering—she needed to call Maggie and ask her friend directly—she said, "What if someone promised Danvers a full-time position if he could make their bad example happen?"

Andre was nodding. "It's possible. But I bet if Danvers got the idea from someone at Blackgate, it was more subtle than that. If anyone got wind of this kind of setup, it would destroy the company."

"Well, they probably hoped that Connors was so drugged up, he'd never put it together that Danvers had pushed him into it," Chelsie suggested. "It's been a year and he's just now figuring it out."

"Or they expected him to die that day," Scott said. "Think about it. How many mass shootings like this end with the shooters in custody?

Usually they end up dead, either by their own hand or 'suicide by cop.' Or because they refuse to surrender."

They all went silent and, slowly, Chelsie found herself nodding. "If he'd stuck around any longer, you guys would have been there. And if he hadn't surrendered when he was pulled over..."

"Still, whether or not he thought Connors would be around to talk, if Danvers is alone in this idea, what's his guarantee he gets anything out of it? It's a huge risk for Danvers if he's got no promise of any personal gain," Scott said. "I hate to say it, but Chelsie's conspiracy idea is sounding more and more plausible."

"I never actually suggested a *conspiracy*," Chelsie protested.

"How many people does it take to make a conspiracy?" Andre joked.

"Well, I'll tell you what we do know for sure," Scott said. "We need to talk to the case agents about this angle and we definitely need to find Danvers."

"WHO'VE YOU GOT?" Scott asked, stretching his arms over his head.

Chelsie tried to keep her eyes on his face and not on the way his movement made his T-shirt stretch across his chest. She'd made herself a promise. She wasn't going to let all this close contact with Scott lessen her resolve not to repeat her mistake.

And she knew it was a mistake. It would fizzle out, but not before rumors got out at work. One way or another, she'd end up hurt. It was best not to go down that road.

She'd been doing well, too, until she'd decided she could handle sitting close to Scott on the couch. He'd reached for her locket, and then taken her hand, and every effort she'd been making at pretending she was unaffected was over. And he hadn't even meant anything by it—he'd merely been trying to do his job and look after her when he'd brought her along, safely behind him, to see why Andre had called for them.

"Uh, too many options," she said when Scott stared expectantly.

She threw her pen on the kitchen table and rubbed her eyes. She and Scott had been researching possible connections between Danvers and the McCord-Siler bill all day. She'd borrowed Andre's laptop since her own was still in her apartment. Scott had taken on researching any potential link to the senators or their staffers. She'd gotten Blackgate.

Andre had thrown in his own theories for a while, then returned to the treadmill. He'd been working out ever since, moving from the treadmill to the living room and leaving her and Scott alone.

"I can't find any obvious connection, but it's not like I have access to phone or email records, so it's hard to track. I'm focusing on motive and opportunity. But honestly, there are a lot of possibilities. The most likely is the CEO, Mark Rubenstein."

"Hmm." Scott frowned. "He'd have the most

to gain, but he's also got the most to lose. And he's pretty high profile. Probably even more than the senators, because except when they're in session or up for reelection, which they weren't at the time of the shooting, neither one of them's in the public eye that much."

"Yeah, and honestly, Rubenstein seems mostly on the up-and-up. His company got some bad press from that incident a few years ago—"

"With the employee who fired on Afghan civilians. I remember."

"But Rubenstein got in front of that pretty fast. Whoever handles his PR knows what they're doing."

"What about a connection to Danvers?" Scott leaned toward Chelsie, distracting her.

There was something about the way he looked at a woman… She abruptly cut off the thought. That ability, making a woman feel she was the only one he saw, was what made Scott such a player.

Maggie had always joked that her brother

treated dating like a sport. And, having no idea of Chelsie's history with him, she'd commented more than once in the past few months that Scott seemed to be going for some kind of dating record lately. So, his night with her couldn't have meant that much to him.

She couldn't allow herself to forget that, no matter how many questions he asked about her life. No matter how he looked at her, with understanding and concern, when she talked about her mom's death.

She cleared her throat and turned her attention back to the laptop, even though there was nothing on her screen she needed to read. "Other than Danvers doing some contract work for Blackgate, I can't find a specific tie to Rubenstein. And I can't find any connection at all to Connors."

"Yeah, I'm not seeing any link to Connors, either, in the senators' camps. Except, of course, that they spun his shooting spree like mad when they were pushing for this bill to go through. Apparently it worked."

"I heard the arguments for the bill using Connors. It seemed like they jumped on that as soon as it happened. But I never thought—"

"I didn't, either," Scott said. "But Andre is right. Digging into it now, it's pretty clear that if Connors hadn't killed those people last year, this bill never would have made it through the Senate. No chance at all."

"Okay, so which of them has the most to gain?" Chelsie asked.

"McCord, definitely. He's up for reelection soon and until this bill got new life, it seemed like his time in the Senate was coming to an end. Now the polls are showing him pretty even."

"You think McCord himself would work with Danvers? Does it seem like he knew Danvers?"

"No and no. But there's someone in McCord's camp who *does* know Danvers." Scott turned his laptop toward her, displaying a photo of a dour-looking man in his forties. His blue eyes were intense, almost angry, and his shoulders barely fit in the frame because they were so huge. His clothes said money, but his size, posture and haircut screamed military background.

"He served with Danvers?" Chelsie asked.

"Nice guess. But no. Liam Hart has been out of the military for more than a decade, since before Danvers joined up. They're nine years apart in age, but they grew up in the same neighborhood."

Chelsie raised her eyebrows. "That can't be coincidence."

"That's what I'm thinking."

"What does Hart do for McCord?"

"He's the guy's key advisor."

"So if McCord loses his reelection bid, Hart is out of a job."

"Exactly. And this is a relatively new career path for Hart. If McCord loses this election, Hart probably won't have an easy time finding another political job, at least not one so important. McCord hired him two years ago when he cleaned house, trying to revamp his image. He knew Hart's father and decided to give the guy a chance. It appears to have been a pretty big salary boost for Hart." Scott raked a hand through his hair, mussing it up and making Chelsie want to run her fingers through it, too. "Now, we just have to prove he was involved."

"Any ideas? All we have is speculation. We're not getting any warrants on theories."

"No kidding. I think our best move is to find Danvers."

"How?" Chelsie stood, tired of sitting hunched over a laptop for so many hours and frustrated from the lack of progress. Sure, they had a suspect, but they were stuck in this safe house, which didn't make it easy to conduct an investigation. Not that they were assigned to the case to begin with.

Scott's eyes followed her as she arched her back, trying to ease out the kinks in her neck. Swallowing down the sudden lump in her throat, she turned her eyes to the floor. But it didn't matter. She could still feel him watching her.

"You've got to stop doing that," she burst out.

"What?" His voice was all innocence, but he stood, moving closer to her, and she could see he knew exactly what she meant.

Forcing down the sudden, ridiculous urge to giggle like a schoolgirl, Chelsie used her best FBI glare. The one that said she might have a willowy, unthreatening frame, but it would be best not to underestimate her.

She'd intended for Scott to back down, but if anything, the desire in his eyes intensified.

He reached out and ran his hand down her bare arm "Stop wanting you?" he asked softly. "I don't think I can do that."

She snatched her arm away, feeling panic rise up. Her track record at resisting him was abysmal. "I don't do meaningless sex," she hissed. "You were an exception. A mistake."

Anger and something else—was it hurt?—crossed his face. "It wasn't meaningless."

"We barely know each other, Scott."

"And whose fault is that?"

"Come on. Talking wasn't exactly what you were pushing for when you asked me to leave the bar with you."

"No, I guess not," he replied tonelessly. "Maybe you're right. That was a mistake." He shook his head, looking vaguely disappointed in her, and left the kitchen.

And even though she'd been the one to say *he* was a mistake first, his words stung.

Why did she keep doing this to herself? She'd always treated romantic relationships the way she'd treated her career path before she'd found the FBI. She never seemed to know quite what she was looking for until she found it.

But until Scott, what she'd found had always been guys who wanted relationships. Guys she could talk to without arguing all the time. Guys who were easy to like. Guys who were easy to leave when the inevitable end came.

Chelsie sat down, surprised at the direction of her thoughts. She wanted a long-term relationship. Didn't she?

She'd always assumed that just like with her career, one day she'd eventually stumble on to the right guy and she'd somehow know it. But maybe she was so busy assuming it wasn't going to work out from the start that she never gave anyone a fair chance.

Not that it applied to Scott. He'd never even been a possibility for a real relationship.

If the FBI had taught her anything, it was that the best predictor of future behavior was past behavior. If she had the luxury of knowing a target's history before trying to negotiate during her training, it had given her the upper hand every time. And that theory didn't only apply to criminals. It applied to everyone.

When it came to Scott, it meant once a player, always a player.

With that, a realization hit her and Chelsie raced into the living room, where she found Andre doing what had to be his millionth one-handed pushup and Scott sitting silently on the couch.

"We need to dig into Danvers's history," she announced.

"Haven't we been doing that?" Scott asked, his gaze cold and impersonal.

Trying not to let it bother her, she turned to Andre, who'd stopped his insane workout and was staring at her expectantly.

"Danvers's ex-wife said he always needed time alone after he returned from a tour, right?"

"Right," Scott answered.

"So, it sounds like he didn't simply lock himself in the bedroom until he felt like returning to civilian life. He went somewhere. Somewhere off the grid, if his wife's answers to the case agents are at all accurate."

Scott nodded slowly as Andre got to his feet. "Do we know where?"

"Let's find out."

"I THINK I found it," Chelsie said, looking up from her perch at the kitchen table.

Scott hurried around the table and leaned over her shoulder to read the computer screen. It showed the deed information for property in Virginia. He nodded, hopeful, as he noted the location. It was in a northern Virginia town used mostly for hunting lodges. A good place to hide away without anyone noticing.

He scanned the rest of the document, and at the top he saw it. "The cabin belongs to Danvers?"

Chelsie shook her head, turning in her chair so she could look at him. Her eyes were a little too wide, and such a perfect shade of blue. As he stared, she coughed and glanced down. "Not *that* Danvers. The cabin belongs to Mike's uncle."

"Nice find." Scott reached around her to move the laptop so he could see the screen better, and she pressed back into her chair, avoiding his touch.

He gritted his teeth and ignored her reaction. She could keep pretending there was nothing between them, but he was going to convince her otherwise. He just needed a new approach.

She believed all he'd wanted from her a year ago was one night. And he'd finally realized his mistake back then—taking her home with him instead of asking her on a real date—was costing him now.

If she was resisting him because she thought all he was after was another one-night stand, he'd have to show her he wanted more. And try to ignore the sour feeling he got whenever he thought of tying himself down to anyone. It felt a little too much like terror.

Which was absurd. Just because he didn't usually go for serious didn't mean he'd *never* done it. Sure, it had been a long time, but that didn't mean he couldn't start again now. He always figured he'd settle down eventually, but he'd never really thought about when that might be.

It had always seemed like a distant idea that would be simple when the time came.

He could crab walk across a ladder stretched between two high-rise buildings with no safety. He could rappel out of a helicopter from thirty feet. He could scale a twenty-foot wall without a harness, ride a skiff in choppy ocean water with pirates shooting at him, take down a terrorist at close range with his bare hands. He'd done all of it in his time at HRT. So why did one white-collar crime Special Agent scare him so much?

He didn't question whether it was worth trying for more with her. His last serious relationship may have been so long ago he barely remembered it, but the thought of *not* having something real with Chelsie was scarier than changing his ways.

The problem was, he knew she'd never believe him if he told her what he wanted. He was going to have to prove it. Which meant he needed to get her to give him a chance.

He turned his attention back to the deed. "This seems like a pretty good hiding spot. Too bad the case agents didn't dig a little deeper."

Chelsie shrugged. "Their focus is finding Connors. But who knows, it could be as simple as Connors and Danvers being in this together. Maybe I was wrong and Connors was spinning it to try to lay blame elsewhere."

He raised his eyebrows at the complete lack of conviction in her voice. "Anything's possible." He straightened, reaching for his cell phone. "But I think you were right all along, Chelsie. Something much bigger than Connors and Danvers is happening here." He started dialing. "Time to find out what it is."

Chapter Eleven

The raid was scheduled to happen in less than an hour.

Chelsie chewed on her fingernails as she paced back and forth in her ten-by-ten–foot bedroom at the safe house. The cabin owned by Mike Danvers's uncle was four hours north of them. By the time Scott had informed the case agents about the cabin and they'd gotten the necessary paperwork in order, another day had passed. But within the hour, the case agents—accompanied by a handful of HRT snipers in case Connors was nearby, too—would be at the cabin. And she would still be here, hiding.

She'd been on a white-collar crime squad for a year now. Money-wise, squads like hers handled some of the biggest cases in the Bureau. And the white-collar stuff sometimes led them to unexpected connections—things like black-market trafficking, cyberespionage and terrorism. It was an important position. Most of the time, it was interesting and challenging. But sitting on the sidelines today suddenly made her miss what she'd given up.

The FBI would have let her return to negotiating. She'd been the one to back out and to request a switch to a new squad. Something that seemed safe. Something where, if she made a mistake, lives weren't usually at stake.

At the time, it had seemed like the right thing to do. Even now, she wasn't sure she'd made a bad choice. No matter how anyone sugarcoated it, people had died that day. And it had been her job to prevent that.

What if she *had* gone back and she'd failed again? Would she be able to live with herself?

At least in white-collar crime, that kind of fear wasn't keeping her up at night.

Even if she'd stayed, she wouldn't have been going to the cabin today. They wouldn't need a negotiator. Either Mike Danvers was innocent and in hiding from his crazy friend, or he was involved to one degree or another. Either he'd come in peacefully or he'd come out shooting. With a case like this—and with a guy like Danvers who had a military background, a soldier's mentality and was off the grid for a reason—it was going to go very well or very badly. She didn't see much chance of anything in between.

No, they wouldn't have needed a negotiator today. But they had taken HRT snipers. And if Scott hadn't been here babysitting her, he probably would have been one of them.

She glanced at her closed bedroom door. As far as she knew, he and Andre were still in the living room together, waiting on the call from the case agents to find out what had happened. But she knew where they both wanted to be right now—it was an HRT agent's style, to always want to be in the center of the action.

Selfishly, she was glad they were here instead. Not because she was worried about herself; she truly believed that Connors wasn't after her. But because she hated the idea of Scott in the line of fire. Which was ridiculous, since that was his full-time job. To put himself in danger to save others.

That wasn't going to change anytime soon, whether they were involved or not. Which, she reminded herself, they never would be.

She looked down at the phone in her hand. She had to stop stressing about things she had no control over. Either she'd find a way to resist Scott and they'd go their separate ways or she wouldn't and she'd end up in bed with him again. Sometimes, it was hard to remember why that was a bad idea.

As for Danvers, either he was at the cabin or he wasn't. Either he could help them find Connors and the FBI's requirement that she stay in protective custody with Scott would be over, or he couldn't. There was nothing she could do about it either way.

But there was something else she needed to do, something she'd been thinking about since yesterday. Glancing once more at the closed door, Chelsie dialed.

"Chelsie, hi." Maggie Delacorte answered on the second ring, and despite her easy greeting, tension vibrated underneath.

"Hey, Maggie." Suddenly Chelsie doubted what she was doing. Scott was going to be pissed when he found out she'd called his little sister after he'd claimed nothing was wrong. But he'd been lying, no question there. And Maggie was her friend.

"What's going on? You haven't gone off anywhere without my brother, have you?"

"No," Chelsie said, embarrassed. Scott had told his sister about her sneaking off? Or had Ella? "I'm calling because…well, listen, you can tell me it's none of my business if you want, but I've overheard Scott calling you a few times. And I'm worried about you. Is everything okay?"

Before Maggie could reply, Chelsie rushed on, "If you need Scott, I'm honestly fine. And I'm sure the Bureau can get someone else to cover anyway."

"Yeah, try getting my brother to back out of the job he volunteered for. Good luck with that."

Scott had asked to be the one protecting her? The news rattled around in Chelsie's brain, and she sat back on the uncomfortable bed. She'd assumed he'd been assigned it, assumed he'd come unwillingly, given the way she'd rejected him six months earlier. Why would he want to be on this detail? Was it some misguided sense of responsibility because he'd been there that day, too? Or was there more to it?

The thought made her clutch the phone a little tighter.

"He's got it in his head that he needs to take care of everyone," Maggie continued.

Well, that answered that question. He'd volunteered because he felt responsible. Which was ridiculous. By the time he'd arrived, it had been too late.

The massacre was her failure. Not his.

"Which is why…"

When her friend trailed off, Chelsie reminded herself to focus on Maggie and prompted, "Why what?"

"Chelsie, you're my friend, but this is something I don't like to talk about. I don't want anyone judging me because of what happened to me a long time ago. I've gotten past it, and I can't stand—" She cut herself off.

Before Chelsie could apologize, Maggie continued, "I'm sure you've heard about my history. It's not exactly a secret to agents who've been at the WFO a while. But you've never once tried to sneak a peek at the back of my neck like some agents, or tried to dig around with subtle questions, which is how I know you're truly my friend."

"Maggie, hey, I'm not asking you about that. I just want to make sure everything is okay *now*. You've been acting distracted and…wait, is this about…has something new happened?" She swore. Maggie had asked her not to talk about it. "I'm sorry. You don't have to say. But… do you need your brother? I swear to you, this threat the FBI thinks I'm under? It's not real. I'm not in danger. I don't need Scott here."

Maggie started to reply, but whatever she was going to say was cut off as Chelsie's bedroom door swung open and Scott snapped, "I don't care if you think you need me here or not."

He came toward her and didn't stop until he was inches away. "I'm not going anywhere."

"Told you," Maggie said in her ear, as Scott added, "I came to see if you wanted to listen in. They're fifteen minutes out and they're looping us in to the command truck."

He scowled at her and added, "Why are you telling people you don't need my help?"

As much as she wanted to hear what happened

at the cabin in real time, listening in wouldn't change the outcome. And something else was going on that Scott needed to hear about, Chelsie was sure of it. Whether Maggie was willing to talk to her about it or not, her negotiator training was screaming that Maggie was hiding something big and it had to do with the Fishhook Rapist.

That predator had evaded capture for a decade, and the FBI had been actively searching for him most of that time. If there'd been a new development in the case, there was no messing around.

And she knew Scott. If his sister needed him and was hiding it, he'd beat himself up for not somehow sensing it and helping her anyway. She knew what it felt like to carry around that kind of guilt, and she couldn't let him do that to himself.

She shoved the phone at Scott. "Talk to your sister. She needs you."

Ignoring Maggie's protests coming from the

phone, Chelsie stepped around Scott and walked out of the room, closing the door behind her.

"MAGGIE? WHAT'S GOING ON?" Scott could hear the strain in his own voice and he took a calming breath.

Maggie has a gun and extensive training in hand-to-hand combat, he reminded himself. She wasn't a twenty-one-year-old kid from a small town who'd never faced hardship anymore. She was a trained federal agent with SWAT teammates who would back her up at a second's notice.

But it didn't matter how many times he reminded himself of that. She was still his little sister. And they were close. There was only one thing Maggie might withhold from him right now, for fear that it would distract him.

His knuckles whitened around the phone until they hurt, but Scott couldn't seem to loosen his grip. "He's made contact again?"

"Yes." Maggie's voice was quiet, the way it

only got when they talked about the SOB who'd hurt her.

A familiar fury welled up, until he wanted to hit something until his hands bled. "When?"

"This morning."

"You should have called me." The words were out of his mouth before he could hold them in, and he swore. "Sorry. But, come on, Maggie, don't hide this stuff from me. Did you talk to Ella?"

"I called her right after I talked to the case agents," Maggie said, and he could hear that she was making a conscious effort not to snap at him for being overprotective.

"Another letter?"

"Yes. Same kind of content."

Scott squeezed his eyes shut, trying to stay calm. The same content as the previous letters meant that the Fishhook Rapist's note read like a sickening love letter. When the first one had arrived, six months ago, he'd actually thrown up when he'd read it. The second one had arrived a few months later and sounded pretty much the same.

It broke him up that his sister had to read this stuff, that she still had no closure over the horrible event that had changed her entire life almost ten years ago. But it also terrified him, this sudden contact, because they hadn't needed Ella's profiling skills to decode what it meant. He and Maggie had both known it the moment they'd read the first letter.

The Fishhook Rapist wasn't going to suddenly stop writing Maggie unless he got caught. And since he only surfaced once a year, their window of time when he was most likely to slip up and get caught was small.

He didn't want his sister to have to deal with this for the rest of her life.

He'd joined the FBI because of the pact he, Maggie and Ella had made. But HRT had called to him on a primal level. The ability to physically, personally take down predators like the man who'd hurt his sister was satisfying like nothing else he'd ever done. It helped heal the guilt he still felt over not being there for Maggie, irrational as it was.

The fact that he had so much specialized training and he still couldn't stop the ever-present threat his sister faced, the terror that the Fish-hook Rapist would one day tire of letters and come for Maggie again, ate him up.

"Stop it," Maggie said, and Scott realized he'd gone silent for too long.

"I know what you're doing right now," Maggie said. "You're beating yourself up about a situation you have no control over. You can't stand guard over me every second. You've got to live your life. Your job takes you all over the country, all over the world. And you know I can take care of myself. I didn't call you right away because I didn't want you to freak out when you need to be focused on watching over Chelsie."

"You can—"

"No," Maggie interrupted, knowing him too well. "I'm not going into protective custody with you guys. The FBI would not sanction that, and it's totally unnecessary. I'm *SWAT*, Scott. And besides, Ella and her fiancé have called me practically every ten minutes since they found out. The ringing phone is starting to drive me nuts, but if I don't pick up, I guarantee you that Ella will break every speed limit to get over here. Believe me, I'll be fine."

Scott was suddenly bone tired. It had been ten years. Would this ever end?

"And anyway," Maggie continued, sounding as if she was trying to convince herself as much as him, "this guy is trying to assert power over me the only way he has left. Which is these piti- ful letters. The whole reason he's still on the loose is because he's smart. Too smart to try to come after an armed federal agent. Besides, I'm not his victim type anymore."

That much was true. The Fishhook Rapist went after women who were in their early to midtwenties exclusively. The reminder loos- ened the knot in his chest a tiny bit.

"Okay, but if there's any reason to think—"

"I'll be fine," Maggie interrupted. "Go listen to the raid."

"You come first, Maggie," he said. "Which means I'm going to be calling you several times a day, too. You don't answer and you should expect Bobby breaking down your door to check on you."

"Bathtub Bobby?"

Scott managed a laugh. "Andre told you about Bobby sleeping in his bathtub?"

"Yeah. Seriously, I don't want you worrying about me. Focus on looking after Chelsie. I was going to call you later and let you in on what's happening, but I don't want to distract you from your job."

"Never happen, Maggie. And if you change your mind about wanting to join us, I'll convince the paper pushers to approve it. I promise."

"I'll be fine," Maggie repeated. "I'll call

you later. Go find out what's going on with Connors."

"Okay. Call me," Scott reminded her.

"Yeah, yeah. Talk to you later, big brother."

Scott hung up the phone, and stared down at it, feeling completely useless.

More than ever, he wished he was at that cabin, kicking in the door and going after the guy who might have set this whole thing with Chelsie in motion.

But hopefully the case agents and his HRT teammates had gotten lucky. Maybe Danvers was in custody now, and already blabbing about where they could find Connors. Maybe it would all be over soon.

Going into the living room, hoping he'd catch the end of the raid, he found Andre and Chelsie staring at each other with matching incredulous expressions.

"What happened?"

They turned toward him. Andre shook his head, and Chelsie told him, "We were too late."

Disappointed, he asked, "Danvers wasn't there?"

"Danvers was there. But when they arrived, he was already dead."

Chapter Twelve

"Who killed him?" Scott asked.

"There was no signed confession," Andre said drily.

Scott sent Andre a dirty look. When Chelsie glanced up, she seemed nervous, probably because she'd butted in with his sister. "The agents finished sweeping the area immediately around the cabin. No obvious signs anyone else was staying with Danvers. It seems more likely that someone tracked him down."

"How was he killed?"

"Bullet to the head," Andre said. "Close quarters. Not a long-distance kill."

"Well, that would be too obvious," Scott said.

Andre nodded. "Yeah, I agree. This seems like payback. Connors definitely thought he had a reason to go after Danvers. And he admitted to us that he was hunting down Danvers."

"He wanted answers," Chelsie argued. "Not revenge."

"Maybe he didn't like the answers he got," Scott said. "He could've questioned Danvers, didn't like what Danvers had to say and killed him. If he'd shoot a bunch of people he'd never even met to make some kind of point, then why not someone he thought had betrayed him?"

"Could be," Chelsie said. "Or maybe it was whoever gave Danvers the idea in the first place. What if that third person was trying to kill Connors at the community center and also tracked Danvers down at the cabin? Someone trying to clean up all the loose ends."

"It's possible," Andre said. "But the right answer is usually the most straightforward. And if it *was* someone else shooting at Connors at the community center, how did he find out Connors would be there?"

"I'm not sure, but I thought you agreed with me that the shooter was probably aiming at Connors?"

"I said it was possible," Andre repeated. "If that was the case, it means the person followed either Connors or Ella to the scene."

Scott felt himself pale, but Andre was quick to point out, "It was most likely Connors he followed. This guy—if he exists—followed Connors to the community center, couldn't hit him, but realized Connors was searching for Danvers. So, he followed Connors until he found Danvers, then went in and killed Danvers at the cabin."

"And Connors did what while this was happening? Watch?" Chelsie asked.

"Connors is one guy," Andre said. "Unless Connors went straight in and confronted Danvers immediately, it would be easy for someone with training to slip past him. He has no spotter. He has to sleep."

Scott nodded, thinking of the way HRT set up sniper hides—spots where they concealed themselves from their targets. There was always one person designated as sniper and another as the spotter. Andre was right; Connors had to sleep eventually. "Following Connors and then sneaking past him when he stopped to take a combat nap is actually a pretty viable option for someone with military training," he told Chelsie, who looked skeptical.

"Connors is trained to locate the target and conduct surveillance before he makes a move," Andre said. "If he's sticking to what he's used to, he'd check the cabin out and confirm Danvers was there, then set up a hide to watch the place. Make sure there was no one else around before he made any kind of move."

Chelsie opened her mouth, no doubt to argue, so Scott added, "Especially if he hadn't decided what he planned to do. If he was being honest with us and he wanted information from Danvers, the smart thing to do would be to locate Danvers, watch for a day to confirm Danvers's routine and make sure no one else was with him, then go in. Danvers was military, too, so Connors would have to anticipate the possibility of a prolonged interrogation. Getting some sleep before he went in would be in his best interest."

"And then someone else slipped past him and killed Danvers?" Chelsie asked. She sounded dejected. "I don't know. That seems unlikely, doesn't it?"

He and Andre were both shaking their heads, but she continued, "I do believe Connors when he said he thinks someone got Danvers to set him up to do the original shooting. But maybe Connors went inside and Danvers told him who set all this in motion, then Connors took out Danvers and is now after that person."

"That's possible, too," Scott agreed. "But our most likely suspect in McCord's camp has military training. He could have slipped past Connors if he was careful."

"Liam Hart," Chelsie said. "The senator's key advisor."

"So does Mark Rubenstein," Scott added. "He's a less likely suspect, but he was spec ops. He hasn't been out of the military as long. Even though he owns Blackgate, when he first started it, he actually went overseas with his employees. Really, any of them has the skill set," he said, frustrated.

Not only was their best lead gone, but the manner of his death didn't point to any one suspect. "Let's ask the case agents to send us time of death as soon as the ME figures it out. We need to check on Rubenstein's and Hart's alibis."

They needed to wrap this up. Find Connors, figure out if there really was a conspiracy or if it was a product of Connors's damaged mind.

Because Scott needed to get home. He needed Chelsie out of danger so he could focus on helping his sister. Not that there was much he could do, besides be close in case she needed him.

He was itching for action. And not the kind that would put someone far away, in the scope of his rifle. He needed some up-close-and-personal action, like the chance to personally knock Connors down and click handcuffs on his wrists. Like the chance to forcibly take down the Fishhook Rapist.

Scott stood up, anxious to act. "What else do we know?"

Andre shook his head. "That's it. The case agents will update us once they've processed the scene."

"Please tell me you have your portable bag in your car," he said to Andre.

Andre got up, understanding on his face. "Yeah. I could go for that myself. I'll grab it."

Chelsie glanced back and forth between Scott and Andre's retreating form. "Portable bag?"

"Punching bag," Scott clarified. "It's smaller than a typical bag, but assignments occasionally take us to some random place for months, while we sit around waiting for the green light. We've ended up in some pretty barren spots. Andre started carrying workout gear in his car. I should have thought about it earlier."

Chelsie got slowly to her feet, looking tentative. "Scott. I want to apologize if I overstepped by calling Maggie. It's just that she's my friend, and I couldn't stand the thought of being the one to keep you here if she needs you."

"There's nothing I can really do right now," Scott said, although it killed him to admit it.

"Are you sure? Because—"

Scott cut her off. "I'm sure." Unable to stop himself, he reached out and smoothed his fingers over the lines that had appeared on her forehead. "Maggie's okay."

He could see her pupils dilate at his touch. He didn't move his fingers from her face, but instead slid them slowly down her cheek, liking the way her eyes widened. She swayed toward him and suddenly the only distraction he wanted right now was her.

He'd intended to keep a respectable distance until the protection was over, then woo her the old-fashioned way, and this time not give up merely because she said *no* to a few dates. But the lure of having her in his arms right now was too strong.

Scott swore, then slipped his hand to her waist and hauled her toward him, covering her surprised yelp with his mouth. He didn't have to coax her lips open, because as soon as his mouth touched hers, she found his tongue with hers, kissing him back as though she'd been just as desperate for his touch.

She slid even closer, getting up on her tiptoes and putting her arms around his neck. Her fingers stroked over his neck, sending sparks of desire through him.

He mumbled his approval into her mouth and moved his hands under the back of her T-shirt, over the curve of her waist, loving the silky smoothness of her skin. He moved his lips from hers long enough to sweep the T-shirt up over her head and onto the floor.

In response, she pulled at the top of his T-shirt, dragging it up inch by inch, until his bare stomach was pressed against hers. The Glock holstered at her hip bumped him as he helped her, taking off his own T-shirt so he could feel the swell of her breasts over the top of her bra pressed against his chest.

She said something unintelligible into his mouth, and he started inching toward the door of the living room with her, the only thought on his mind to get her to a bed. As he was backing through the doorway, he slammed into a hard object.

He realized it was Andre's punching bag at the same time Chelsie gave an embarrassed squeak and darted away from him, snatching her T-shirt off the floor.

Scott turned, cursing under his breath. He'd been so caught up with Chelsie, he'd totally forgotten where they were. He should have moved faster, gotten her into a bedroom before Andre came back and broke the spell Chelsie seemed to have fallen under. He could hear her behind him, hurrying to put her T-shirt back on.

"Sorry, man," Andre said quietly, backing out of the room fast.

"Andre," Chelsie's voice rang out.

Scott glanced back and saw that Chelsie was dressed again, her arms crossed protectively over her chest, and her cheeks flaming.

She walked by, careful not to touch him, and told Andre, "Sorry about that."

"Don't worry about it," Andre said. "I'll hang out in the kitchen for a—"

"It's fine," Chelsie interrupted. "It won't happen again."

Before Scott could say anything at all, Chelsie rushed past him and down the hall to her room, alone.

WHAT WAS SHE THINKING?

What was it about Scott that destroyed every

bit of resistance she possessed? She'd never been like this with anyone, not even with serious ex-boyfriends. When it was over, it was over. She'd never gone for the one-last-time argument, never been drawn back to an ex because she was lonely or missing what they'd had. When they severed ties, that was the end.

She'd never been one to linger in regrets. She liked clean breaks.

Why was Scott different?

Chelsie removed her holster, Glock and handcuffs and set them on the side table, then dropped onto the bed, lying with one hand over her eyes. It was because she had real feelings for Scott, she realized. She probably always had, but hadn't wanted to admit it, even to herself. And deep down, she regretted not giving him a chance after that first night.

She didn't kid herself about what would have happened. Scott wasn't suddenly going to change his ways for her. She wasn't some romantic fool.

But perhaps she should have let the attraction run its course, let herself have as much as she could with him for as long as it lasted. Being with Scott the past week, getting to know him a little better, made her certain that when the inevitable end came, she'd wish it wasn't over, probably wish she'd never started anything at all. But maybe it would have been worth it.

Even if being with him brought all her feelings of failure back to the surface? The feelings it had taken her a year to bury as deep as she could? The thought made her nauseated. But with Connors on the run, that self-doubt was bubbling back up already. Would another fling with Scott really make it worse?

"Chelsie?"

A soft knock at the door followed and Chelsie sat up fast. "Yeah?"

There was exasperation in Scott's tone as he asked, "Can I come in?"

"Sure." She fidgeted as he came through the door and closed it behind him.

"I think I should apologize," he said as he came toward her, until she had to stand up and step away from the bed so she wouldn't grab him and tug him down with her.

"No, it was my—"

"I'm not actually sorry it happened," he cut her off. "But it was bad timing." He broke into that grin that made her feel as if he was imagining all the ways he could make her come. "You're a little hard to resist."

She squirmed, trying to hold eye contact. "Ditto."

"Well, good. Because I was hoping once we're out of this safe house, I could take you out for dinner."

"I think we should…"

He stepped a little closer. "Give me a chance, Chelsie."

She sucked in a breath and moved backward, bumping into the bed and almost falling, but catching herself in time. "Not here."

Smile lines formed around his eyes, like he

was trying not to laugh at her. "No, takeout pizza doesn't count as dinner."

"I meant..." Was she really going to do this? Chelsie took a deep breath and decided *yes*. A fling with Scott wasn't a relationship; it wouldn't be a reminder that sucked her back into that despair she'd felt after the massacre. It would be a distraction, and maybe she could hold on to a memory of him that didn't end in bloodshed. She felt her face heat up another hundred degrees or so as she said, "I meant that when this is over, I'll go home with you."

He shook his head. Reaching a hand out and twirling a strand of her hair around his finger, he replied, "Dinner. At least five dates before I'll put out."

She gave a surprised laugh. "What?"

"Okay. Fine." He grinned wider. "Since I'm sure you're going to wear me down with those negotiator skills, three dates. But that's my final offer." He dropped her hair and moved in.

That fast, Chelsie's determination to at least

wait until they weren't at the safe house with Andre in the next room evaporated. She stared up at him, waiting for his lips to press against hers, certain he couldn't be serious about taking her out on real dates first.

Instead, he lowered his face slowly, his lips barely brushing hers as he whispered, "We have a deal?"

Clutching fistfuls of his T-shirt in her hands, she nodded before she'd really thought it through.

Only then did he kiss her. Instead of the explosion of passion she was used to with Scott, this kiss was gentle and slow. His mouth moved with precision, until her hands and feet tingled and she was desperate for more, but didn't want to break the romantic spell he'd cast over her.

When he finally pulled away, she stared up at him, dazed, her heart thumping a nervous, excited beat. Was he serious? Did he actually want something real?

She was going to find out. If he could truly

make it three dates without trying to get her into bed, then she'd know. And if he was willing to take a chance on her, she could do the same. Maybe her feelings for him didn't *have* to be tied into that horrible day. She felt a slow smile grow.

An answering smile lit Scott's face. "What?"

"You really volunteered for my protective detail?"

"Yeah." He looked surprised. "Of course I did."

"Why?"

Instantly, his expression turned serious. "Why do you think, Chelsie? I couldn't let anything happen to you."

She felt warm all over and knew she was staring up at him like a lovesick teenager, but she couldn't help it.

She'd never been the kind of person to separate love and sex, and her night with Scott had been an aberration. An event that had seemed as wrong as it had felt right. One night with someone wasn't enough time to develop a real connection, but since she'd been locked in close quarters with him over the past week, she'd gotten to see so much more of who he was. And she liked him way too much.

Had she known all along this would happen? That if she gave him a chance, she'd fall for him and he'd eventually walk away and it would be so much worse?

Now that she'd finally made her choice to let herself have whatever she could with Scott for as long as it lasted, had she set herself up for heartbreak?

"ALIBIS?" SCOTT ASKED.

He and Andre were sitting on the living room couch, laptops in front of them, looking serious. Andre's phone was lying on the seat between them, so he could pick it up as soon the case agents called back with more information.

Chelsie sat across from them, trying to focus. Ever since the situation in LA with her supervisor, she'd sworn off dating other agents. It was one of her few rules. Unfair as it was, as a woman, she knew what it could do to her reputation.

Some nagging voice in the back of her mind told her that was just an excuse—that Scott wasn't her boss, and it was a totally different situation—but she ignored it. She didn't want to risk her job in white-collar crime, even if it didn't get her pulse going like negotiation.

So, she'd have to keep her relationship with Scott a secret. For as long as it lasted, she'd ask him to keep it low-key. Obviously, Ella already knew, but she wouldn't tell anyone, except possibly Maggie. And hopefully Maggie would forgive her when things eventually fizzled out.

She knew whatever she and Scott were about to start had an expiration date; she just didn't want to dwell on that part. Because the idea of dating Scott, actually *dating* him, filled her with the sort of anticipation she hadn't felt about anything since before the massacre.

"...you think, Chelsie?"

"What?" Chelsie blinked, trying to come up with what Scott had said, but it was no use. "Sorry. What did you ask?"

Scott gave her an amused glance, as if he knew exactly what had her so distracted since he'd made his suggestion in her room a few hours earlier. "I said, what do you think about trying a ruse? I don't want Hart to realize we're onto him if he's guilty."

Get it together, Chelsie told herself, sitting straighter in her chair and trying to focus on the problem at hand. "Well, we don't even have an official time of death yet."

"No, but rigor hadn't set in, so it was within the past day," Andre said. "And when I called and asked for Hart at his office, his secretary said he was out this week."

"For all we know, he's there, but not taking calls," Scott said.

"Okay," Andre said. "What about Rubenstein?"

Scott shook his head. "I couldn't get past his assistant. They weren't giving me any information or letting me talk to the guy without a scheduled call. Obviously, I'm not giving my real name or mentioning that I'm FBI. No need to tip him off if he's involved."

"So, we don't have an alibi for either one," Chelsie summed up.

"Nope," Scott said. "We should be able to look into Danvers's call history and emails soon, though. Hopefully that'll give us the connection."

"The case agents will be able to do that," Andre corrected. "Not us."

"They'll share." Scott sounded certain. "They want the help on this. They're catching enough heat about Connors still being loose."

"Not technically their responsibility," Andre said.

"True, but they're working with the US Marshals to bring Connors in. And they're the ones expected to provide some insight into why he went after one of our agents." Scott glanced at Chelsie.

"Connors wanted my help," Chelsie answered simply. She was certain of it now, even though it was an odd choice for Connors to make. Because she might want to uncover the truth about who else was involved, but she still wanted Connors back in prison. The sooner the better.

Especially since being out of protective custody meant going on a real date with Scott Delacorte. Chelsie bit back a grin, already craving the feel of his hand in hers.

"Yeah, well, the case agents don't buy that," Andre said.

"They don't?" Chelsie was surprised. "Even after Danvers's death? They don't think it's odd that a guy Connors claimed set him up is suddenly dead?"

"They think it's a sign Connors is back to killing," Andre said. "Which is the most logical conclusion."

Chelsie frowned. "I suppose that's true."

"It could be that simple," Scott said. "Rubenstein and Hart might have absolutely nothing to do with this. It's possible the conspiracy was all in Connors's mind. Or it could have been Danvers's plan to set Connors up, all on his own."

"Well, if it was Connors who killed Danvers, we'll probably find out soon enough whether anyone else was involved," Chelsie said.

Scott nodded. "Because that person will probably turn up dead soon, too."

Chapter Thirteen

"No one else has turned up dead yet," Scott announced when Chelsie walked into the kitchen the next morning.

He held out a cup of coffee to her, wearing worn jeans, a T-shirt and the kind of smile she wouldn't mind seeing every morning as soon as she woke up.

Chelsie took the cup, nodding gratefully, and tried to banish the ridiculous thought. If she let herself, she could fall way too hard for Scott, and that would make things so much worse when it ended.

The panic must have shown on her face,

because Scott suddenly looked concerned. "What's wrong?"

"Uh," Chelsie stammered, "this isn't Andre's coffee, is it?"

Scott laughed. "No, it's safe. I can make a cup of coffee."

"What about breakfast?" The question came out before she thought it through.

His eyes moved over her from head to toe in the capris and T-shirt the cop had packed for her. It was her second day wearing them and she didn't feel remotely sexy, but the way Scott was looking at her, she could have been standing in the kitchen in a negligee.

"Three dates," he reminded her. "And then I'll let you be the judge."

She had a feeling that after three dates, the only thing she was going to want in the morning was a second helping of Scott, but instead of saying that, she nodded. "I'll hold you to it."

She'd meant it as a joke, mostly to hide her

nerves at this new territory they were entering, but he stepped closer.

"I hope so," he said, his voice dropping to a low growl.

He smelled like fresh-ground coffee and some kind of aftershave. And despite the fact that his clothes were on their second wear, too, on him, the rumpled look was sexy.

Realizing she was staring, Chelsie sipped her coffee, hoping it would clear her head. But she swallowed and he was still there, so close that she could set her coffee down, then reach out and grab a fistful of his shirt. Tug him to her and take a sampling of what he was offering for later. Press her lips to his and see how far his determination to wait three dates went. She bit her lip, debating whether she should really do it.

Scott's gaze bored into her, as though he could read exactly what was going through her mind.

"We've got the official go-ahead," Andre's voice carried as he walked into the kitchen. He slowed to a stop as he saw them, standing close and staring at each other as if they wanted to rip off each other's clothes.

At least she assumed that was the expression on her face. It was definitely the expression on Scott's.

"Want me to come back later?"

Scott rolled his eyes at his partner. "Don't be a smart-ass."

Andre grinned back, then looked at the mug in Chelsie's hands. "Coffee?"

"Help yourself," Scott said. "And take notes. The way I make it, you couldn't clean drains with it."

"Ha ha," Andre said, pouring himself a cup of coffee. He took a sip, then added, "A little weak."

"The go-ahead on what?" Chelsie asked, a bit relieved to have a distraction from Scott.

"Danvers's autopsy is complete. His death was ruled a homicide, obviously. But now we can start investigating. The good news is, the case agents are still processing the cabin and the surrounding area. They're trying to figure out where the killer came in, where he might have parked, those kinds of logistics. I guess the cabin is pretty remote. Not a lot of obvious methods of entry and exit, so they're hoping to come up with some tire tracks they can match to a vehicle type. They figure that might give them a useful detail to add to Connors's BOLO, help bring him in sooner."

"Assuming it was Connors who killed him," Chelsie said.

"Which they are," Andre said. "But Connors isn't stupid. Unless he's back on painkillers, he didn't leave tire tracks."

"Even if he is back on them," Scott said. "If it was him, he probably wiped his tracks."

"True," Andre agreed. "Those shots a year ago were dead-on, considering how many drugs were in his system."

"Yeah, I remember," Scott said, and the dire

tone of his voice made her glance at him, curious.

His eyes were on her, protective and fierce, and she realized he still wasn't 100 percent certain that Connors wouldn't come after her. And he was worried that Connors's demonstrated skill with a rifle while drugged up proved he'd be impossible to stop when he was totally sober.

Without thinking, she reached out and folded her hand in his. "Connors isn't going to find me here."

Andre looked down at their linked hands, his eyebrows shooting up, and Chelsie blushed and tried to pull her hand free.

But Scott held on tighter, tugged her closer to him. "No, he's not."

So much for her idea of keeping their budding relationship a secret. Not that Andre didn't already know there was way more than a professional bond between them. At least he didn't seem like the gossipy type.

Scott smiled at her, then turned back to his partner. "So, what did we get?"

"The good stuff," Andre replied. "Email and phone records."

"Nice." Scott started moving toward the living room, where he and Andre had left their laptops last night. He didn't let go of her, just walked with her beside him as though it was natural for them to be holding hands. "Let's see if we can link Danvers to Rubenstein or Hart."

"I THINK I'VE got something," Chelsie announced three hours later.

She was sitting cross-legged on the living room chair and Scott wasn't surprised she'd been the first to come up with a possible lead. They'd been passing the two laptops around for the past few hours, to give everyone's eyes a break, but Chelsie had been the most focused. Andre had gotten up three times for refills on his coffee, claiming he had to drink twice as much for the same effect. And Scott had been distracted by Chelsie's long legs crossed in front of her, her bare feet tucked into the edges of the chair. Even her toes were sexy.

Scott tried to shake the kinks out of his shoulders and focus. "What is it?"

"Phone calls. Two of them, a week before the shooting."

"Danvers has got a logical reason to call Rubenstein," Andre reminded her. "Even though he wasn't working for the firm then, he could easily claim it was prejob stuff."

"Sure," Chelsie said, grinning triumphantly. "But does he have a legitimate reason to be calling Hart?"

In unison, Scott and Andre leaned forward. "He called Hart?"

"Yep. Twice. The calls went to Hart's work cell phone. The first one lasted twenty minutes and the second one for ten."

"So, no one can claim a wrong number," Scott mused.

"Well, you said that Danvers and Hart grew

up in the same neighborhood," Andre reminded Scott. "Maybe they're friends."

"There's an age difference, so they didn't go to school together," Scott said. "But they probably *do* know each other. If Hart convinced Danvers to go along with this, he had to have known him. But there was no indication they've had contact recently. And why would Danvers call Hart's work phone instead of his home phone if it was a personal call?"

"Not having seen each other for a while would be perfect for his plan." Chelsie spoke excitedly as she unfolded her legs, turning Andre's laptop so they could see. "That way, there'd be no obvious connection."

"Two phone calls doesn't a murderer make," Scott reminded her, not wanting her to raise her hopes if they were going down the wrong path. After all, the best evidence they had so far that there was a conspiracy was the word of a killer.

"True. But they definitely make me suspicious. It's not beyond the realm of possibility that Hart wanted to create an incident that would help this bill pass, knowing it was the only way to save his boss's, and therefore his own, job. And he knew Danvers, knew he was transitioning into the private sector, and thought he could use him."

"Or Hart was promised a payoff to get the bill to pass and he knew he could guarantee Danvers a job from the company paying him," Andre suggested.

"You think Hart and Rubenstein are both in on it?" Chelsie asked.

"Probably not," Andre replied. "But it wouldn't surprise me if Rubenstein was filling someone's pockets to get the bill passed, with no questions about how it happened."

Chelsie sighed. "Well, we don't have any way to search for that connection."

"Doubt we'd find it if it was there," Andre said, standing and stretching. "I can tell you one thing after reviewing their backgrounds.

Rubenstein is a lot smarter than Hart. He'd be better at hiding his tracks if he was involved."

"And if he was paying someone off and then he discovered he'd funded a massacre, he'd bury those tracks as deep as possible," Scott said.

"We need more than a couple of phone calls, unfortunately," Andre said. "Did anything pop up in the email?"

Scott shook his head. "Not yet." He passed the laptop over to Andre. "But you can take a turn."

"What about bank access?" Chelsie asked.

"We don't have that yet," Andre replied. "But it's a good idea. I'm sure Rubenstein set up overseas accounts if there was a payoff. But looking at some of the messy paper trails Danvers has left, it wouldn't surprise me to find a large deposit in his regular account. We should check it out—maybe we can track it back to Hart."

"What other messy paper trails?" Scott asked.

"Sounds like he was stealing from the military when he was overseas. Minor stuff, but he brags about it over email to someone. Same with an affair he had back when he was married."

Chelsie made a face. "Sounds like a great guy."

"Were there any details about the IED that killed Connors's team?" Scott asked. Although he didn't think Danvers had anything to do with that, if Danvers *had* convinced Connors to plan a massacre, why him? The one person from his old team to survive an ambush, and Danvers set him up to spend the rest of his life in jail—or to be killed on scene? "Did Danvers and Connors have a falling out?"

"Hmm." Andre nodded. "Good point. Let me run a search." He stared intently at the computer for a few minutes, typing away, then finally glanced up. "No, Connors and Danvers emailed after Connors came home. It was sporadic, and Connors is clearly depressed. But those emails do seem normal. What is interesting, though, is another email. He sent one to a different Army buddy, where he implies that Connors only survived because he traded places with someone else in the transport."

"What?" Scott shifted to peer over Andre's shoulder at the laptop.

"It's vague and there's an email the next day backtracking, saying he was drinking when he sent this one, but look." Andre pointed.

"Read it out loud," Chelsie said.

"Wow." Instead of reading Chelsie the nasty letter, Scott paraphrased. "Okay, so apparently Connors was in the back of the vehicle, but he was supposed to be driving when the IED blew. The person who *was* driving was Danvers's best friend in the unit."

"That might be why he chose Connors for this," Chelsie said.

"Sure," Scott agreed, frowning at the email. "Connors was an easy target, already depressed and on a lot of pills. Danvers feels guilty because he'd just transferred out of the unit, so he lived. And his best friend died in Connors's seat."

He looked over at Chelsie. "This is a pretty big sign Danvers could have gone after Connors all on his own."

"Or it made *him* an easy target, too," Chelsie pointed out. "Because he has an obvious grudge."

"Well, why not go straight to the source?" Andre asked. "Skip Danvers altogether?"

"Because Hart didn't know Connors. But he did know Danvers, knew he was trying to get a full-time spot with a private security firm," Chelsie said.

"Right." Scott nodded. "But still, everything we've seen so far makes Danvers seem guilty. All we've got on Hart is theory." Chelsie seemed about to disagree, so he added quickly, "I think there's a good chance you're right, Chelsie. But we need to follow the evidence, not chase theories to the wrong outcome."

"I think—" Andre started, but stopped when his cell phone rang. "It's the case agents." He answered, then punched the speaker button.

"It's Diaz. You've got Delacorte and Russell on the line, too."

"You're not going to believe who we found," Owen Jennings, the lead case agent said, excitement in his voice.

"Liam Hart?" Chelsie guessed.

"Who?" Owen asked. "No, Clayton Connors."

Shocked, Scott looked over at Chelsie. Connors had gotten caught? Did that mean no one else besides Danvers was involved, so after killing him, he'd given himself up? "He turned himself in?"

"Nope. We were searching around the cabin, and we found his—what do you snipers call it?"

"His hide?" Andre guessed.

"Right. His hide. Well, he was there."

"He stayed. Why?"

"After he took Danvers out, he went back to his hide and killed himself."

"What?" Chelsie gasped.

"Clayton Connors is dead. You can pack up and go home. It's over."

Chapter Fourteen

"Clayton Connors did *not* kill himself," Chelsie insisted.

"He was facing the possibility of returning to life in prison," Andre reminded her. "He was good at hiding, but he had to know that eventually we'd catch up to him. Let's say Danvers told him no one else was involved, then Connors killed him. What was left for Connors to do? There'd be no one else to chase after, and only prison waiting for him."

"He did express regret over his actions," Scott said slowly.

"See?" Andre said. "He felt guilty. As he

should. And once he found out his big conspiracy theory was wrong and he only had himself and Danvers to blame, he killed himself instead of going back to jail."

Chelsie dropped her duffel bag at her feet. After the case agent's phone call, they'd gotten the word that the protective custody was over. It was time to leave the safe house and go back to her normal life.

She'd shut herself in her room to pack, and to think. What she'd come up with was the certainty that the case agents were wrong.

"Someone killed him," she insisted stubbornly. "You said yourself that someone with training could slip past Connors."

"Sure. But that same someone would have also had to sneak up on Connors and kill him," said Andre. "That's a much taller order." He shrugged and picked up the bag she'd dropped. "I hate to say it, but I think we let Connors get in our heads with his conspiracy theories."

"Scott?" Chelsie turned to stare at him.

He looked serious and intent, the same expression she imagined him having as he stared through his rifle scope at a hostage taker.

If she was right, whoever was on the other end of that scope didn't stand a chance.

"I agree with Chelsie."

"You do?" she and Andre asked simultaneously.

"It's way too convenient. If Hart was behind this, all his loose ends have been neatly tied up."

"But—" Andre started.

"Besides," Scott talked over his partner, "Chelsie got to Connors at the community center last week. We both saw it."

"Sure," Andre agreed. "Until right before those gunshots came, when I know you were thinking the same thing I was. That he was about to take out Chelsie and himself."

"That's not what was about to happen," Chelsie said.

"Connors identified with Chelsie that day," Scott continued. "He said he came to her to help him find Danvers because he knew she needed closure, too. I think if he was going to kill himself, he would have left her a note."

"Are you serious?" Andre scoffed. "Come on, man. He *murdered* nine people he didn't know. You think he cares enough to leave one FBI negotiator an explanation before he blew his own brains out? That's crazy."

"Not an explanation about why he killed himself. An explanation about what the killing was all about." Scott was looking at her. "You got inside his mind that day. You tell us. Was he suicidal? If Danvers claimed no one else was involved and he murdered Danvers, would he feel so guilty, he'd kill himself, too?"

"Maybe," Chelsie said. "If he believed Danvers. But he was convinced there was more going on. If Danvers died not naming anyone else, I don't think Connors would have stopped digging because I don't think Connors would have bought it. And the more I think about it, the less I believe he would have killed Danvers.

I think he wanted Danvers to pay like he was. Publicly. Same with anyone else involved."

Scott nodded, like her word was the end of it.

How could he have that much faith in her? What had changed since the shoot-out at the community center last week, when he'd called her a fool for falling for Connors's story?

She squinted at him, trying to figure it out, but he was staring pointedly at Andre, seeming to have some kind of wordless conversation. Andre was frowning back at him, like he understood. Apparently, sniper speak didn't involve words.

All along, Scott had insisted she knew how to get into people's minds. But if she was really that good at it, would they be in this position in the first place?

"It's just my opinion," she blurted. "I could be wrong."

Scott spun toward her. "Stop doubting yourself," he snapped. "You were a good negotiator. What's it going to take for you to believe in yourself again?" Before she found her voice, he said, "Come on. Let's get out of here. We're going to keep digging until we find whoever did this. And until then, Chelsie, you're not going home. You're staying with me."

SHE NEEDED TO trust herself. The words Scott had said in the safe house ran over and over in her head like an endless soundtrack as he drove.

She sat in the passenger seat, silent. She hadn't said a word since his announcement she wasn't going home. From the corner of her eye, she sneaked a glance at Scott, but he was staring intently at the road as he drove. He'd been silent the entire ride, too.

They'd be at his house soon and then it would be just the two of them. No Andre to keep things from going too far, no drab Bureau safe house as a constant reminder of why they were with each other at all. Soon, they'd be alone in the place where they'd spent their only night together.

Chelsie tried to ignore that fact and think about the case. Could she trust herself again?

If she was right, then something much bigger than just Connors and Danvers was happening. If she was wrong, then she was wasting everyone's time, and Scott's faith in her would be destroyed.

And Scott's faith in her mattered a lot. More than it should for someone she'd decided she could have a fling with and then walk away from.

Deep down, she knew she was fooling herself about that, but if she admitted it, she might change her mind and back out. And she was finished with hiding from things because they scared her, Scott included. She wanted to make a change, shake off this insecurity that had plagued her since the massacre. But she wasn't sure if she could do it.

Fingering the locket around her neck, Chelsie leaned against the headrest. She sensed that Scott had glanced at her, then back at the road, but she kept staring straight ahead. How did she know if she could trust her own judgment again? Frustration built up. A year ago, she'd never even thought about that. She just did it. Now, she wasn't sure how.

"We're here," Scott said, and she realized the SUV was parked in his garage.

Avoiding his gaze as she unbuckled her seat belt, she muttered, "You know, I'd probably be fine at home. Connors went to my apartment because he wanted my help. Hart has no reason to come after me."

"Well, if he's been following Connors, then he knows Connors talked to you. And if he was shooting last week at the community center, he couldn't hear what Connors said to you."

She stopped in the middle of opening her door. Scott was right about that. "At least he's not as good a shot as Connors," she said, intending it to be a joke, to lighten the mood a little.

"No, he's not a sharpshooter," Scott agreed,

but he didn't sound amused. "But you're still not leaving my sight until we nail this guy."

There were a lot of logistics she was sure he hadn't thought through about that—like the fact that both of them had to return to work soon. But what mattered most right now was whether she really needed to be here at all.

"What if it's not him?" She turned to face him. "I know you believe me." The words seemed to stick in her throat, the wonder of him believing in her more than she did. "But everyone makes mistakes."

Scott nodded. "Everyone does, but you're right this time, Chelsie."

"What changed your mind?"

He frowned, like he was thinking about it, then said, "You sounded so positive when you said Connors wouldn't kill himself. I could see it in your eyes. You were certain. I've gotten that same gut feeling on a job, Chelsie. I understand what it's like to be positive about something, even when the evidence might suggest otherwise. And when it's my specialty, I trust my gut." He shrugged and reached into the backseat to grab both their bags. "Haven't been wrong yet."

"But I have," Chelsie whispered as he slammed the door shut.

She followed him into his house, letting herself look around in a way she hadn't bothered to the last time she was here. She was surprised to find that her memories of his house were not only accurate, but that she remembered more than she'd realized.

He led her through the garage and into the kitchen. She hadn't done more than peek into this room when he'd brought her here before, but she still remembered the blue walls, the stainless-steel appliances, the goofy old picture of him and Maggie and a little girl. She leaned closer, realizing the second girl in the picture must be Nikki. Scott and Maggie appeared to be in their early teens, and Nikki was a toddler, perched in Scott's lap.

"My sisters," Scott said, not glancing back as he continued through the kitchen. "Once this is over, I'll introduce you to Nikki. You'll like her. She's nothing like Maggie and me. A little more thought than action…in a good way. Like you."

Chelsie faltered briefly, and then hurried to catch up. He wanted to introduce her to his family? "Scott?"

"Yeah?" He turned around, looking wary, probably hearing the uncertainty in her tone.

"Let's keep this—" she gestured between them, still not really sure what *this* was "—between us for now, okay?"

Disappointment flashed across his face, then it was gone. "What happened to you agreeing to give me a chance?"

"Listen, we both know—"

"What?" He dropped their bags on the floor, moving forward until he was only inches from her. "What do we both know, Chelsie?"

"I don't want it to become an issue at work."

It was true, but as she said it aloud, it sounded like an excuse. It *felt* like an excuse.

"What does meeting my little sister have to do with work?" Not letting her answer, Scott continued, "Either give me a chance or don't, Chelsie. But you need to stop playing games with me and choose."

Her, play games? He was the one who never stuck with one woman. Angry, she jabbed a finger at his chest. "A year ago—"

"This isn't a year ago," he cut her off. "I've spent the past year trying to get you out of my head and it hasn't worked."

She felt her jaw go slack as he continued, "And I've spent the past week and a half getting to know you better. I want you in my life, Chelsie. So, you need to decide what *you* want. Stop hiding behind one bad case and make a choice! About me, about your career, about everything. Just decide!"

"That's not fair!" she argued, pissed off and fixating on that emotion instead of the other feelings bubbling underneath. Fear that he was right. Excitement that he wanted her in his life. Fear that he'd change his mind if he actually got what he was asking for.

Well, there was only one way to find out about that, she realized. Actually give him a real chance. Try not to assume what they had together had an automatic expiration date. See if she could be happy with him. Could she do it?

As she stared up at him, silent, she realized her internal debate must have been playing out across her face, because he was watching her expectantly.

It was time to stop hedging her bets and go all in.

So, she drew a fortifying breath, then leaned in and kissed him for all she was worth.

Not exactly the answer he was expecting, but even better than he'd been hoping for.

Scott wrapped his arms around Chelsie's waist, and his fingers instantly found their way under the hem of her shirt. Stroking her soft skin, he breathed deep, the smell of her strawberry shampoo like an aphrodisiac.

Her arms locked tight around his neck, and she pushed herself up against him. Her tongue danced in his mouth as she made little impatient noises in the back of her throat.

He could feel every inch of her body through her lightweight capris and thin T-shirt, but it wasn't enough. It wasn't close to enough. Sliding his hands down to the curve of her butt, he lifted her up and she wound her legs around his waist, using the extra height to kiss him more deeply.

Man, this was the best "yes, I'll date you" answer he could possibly have gotten.

Pivoting, he hurried to his bedroom, not opening his eyes as he stroked the inside of her mouth with his tongue and ran his hands over the backs of her thighs until she squirmed. He picked up his pace, kicking open his bedroom door and depositing her in the center of his bed.

She looked good there, smiling up at him, mischievousness in the curve of her lips and warmth in her eyes. When he didn't immediately lower himself on top of her, she curved her finger at him, beckoning.

He stared down at her, smiling, just wanting to watch her for a minute, in his bed, agreeing to be his—what? Girlfriend? When was the last time he'd said that about anyone? When was the last time he'd even wanted that?

But right now, with Chelsie, there was no question. He wanted serious. And he'd do whatever it took to get it.

He ran his eyes over all the places on her lean, strong body he wanted to put his hands and lips. She sat up, hooking her finger in the waistband of his jeans and yanking him down hard.

He laughed, catching his weight on his hands so he wouldn't crush her. Before he'd finished lowering himself slowly on top of her, savoring the expressions crossing her face, she wrapped her legs around him again. She pulled his

T-shirt over his head, and then he couldn't watch her anymore because his eyes rolled back in his head as she arched her back and rolled her body against him.

Suddenly impatient, he yanked her T-shirt off, then paused long enough to unholster both their weapons and set them on the side table. Raised up on his forearms, he paused to admire the swell of her breasts in her light blue bra and then reached down, unsnapping her capris. Since he couldn't get them off with her legs tight around him, he slid his hands into the back of them. Cupping her butt, he angled her against him just right, loving the way she sucked in a breath and grabbed his head, bringing it back down to hers.

He shifted and kissed her more deeply, trying to show her how much he wanted her here, in his life.

Volunteering for that protection detail was the best decision he'd ever made.

He kissed along her jawline, licking her earlobe and then whispered in her ear, "I think you should call in sick for a few days. Let me practice protecting you."

She made a sound somewhere between a laugh and a moan as he slid down her body, kissing his way from her earlobe to her breasts. He ran his hands over her thighs, unhooking them from his waist so he could move over her more easily, so he could slip her capris down her long legs.

When he had them off, he started working his way back up, dropping kisses every few inches as his hands relearned the lines of her body. He slowed at the spot near her hip that he remembered drove her crazy, teasing her with his tongue as her hands curled into fists in his hair.

"I knew you couldn't wait three dates." She laughed breathlessly.

Scott froze, planting his hands on the mattress and lowering his head onto her stomach, his body and mind battling. He'd seen the look in her eyes when he'd promised her three dates before he tried to get her in bed. She hadn't believed him. And right now, he was proving her right. No matter that it wasn't true, he was showing her she was still a fling.

And if he really wanted this to last, he knew he had to convince her that he'd changed.

Swearing, Scott pushed himself off her and drew a deep breath. She was staring up at him, confusion on her face mingled with desire.

"Three dates," he agreed, snatching his T-shirt off the floor and putting it on, then snapping his holster back in place. "You can stay here. I'll sleep in the guest room," he managed. Then, before all his good intentions were overcome by the sight of her in his bed, in her underwear, he fled the room.

Chapter Fifteen

"Are you kidding me?" Chelsie stood in the doorway of his guest bedroom, hands on hips.

Scott groaned and closed his eyes briefly, but it didn't matter. The image of her standing there in nothing but a skimpy blue bra and panties was imprinted on his eyeballs. "Can you put some clothes on?" he asked hoarsely.

She scowled, then insight dawned in her eyes and she stepped closer.

Scott sat up in the bed, where he'd been trying to cool off after leaving Chelsie. As she moved toward him, her eyes wandering over him hungrily, the way he'd looked at her earlier, he thought better of staying on the bed and got to his feet, holding up a hand.

"You wanted me to prove I was serious about you. That's what I'm doing."

Chelsie shook her head. "I never said that."

"Not in so many words. But every time I try for more, you throw the one-night stand in my face. Which was your fault, by the way. I called. You were the one who refused to answer."

She stopped a foot away from him, her hands still on her hips, frowning at him, but the effect was ruined by how little she was wearing.

He tried to keep his eyes on her face, but it kept wandering down. Her legs went on forever, and he knew how soft her skin was. He knew exactly how good her hair felt against his skin as she trailed her lips over his body. He was dying to slide those scraps of fabric off her and pull her down on top of him, remind her how good they could be together.

"You're the one who had the reputation—"

Well, that did it. He eyes went back up to hers,

furious. "What's it going to take for me to prove you're different?"

A fast step forward and he was in her personal space, but instead of bringing her close, like he wanted to, he asked, "Is this actually about me or is it about you, Chelsie? You keep hiding behind this excuse, but have I ever given you reason to think you were a fling? I asked you out for months. I didn't go out with anyone that whole time. Not until you finally convinced me you were never going to say yes!" He sighed, frustrated. "It doesn't matter what I do, does it? You're never going to believe me, because you don't want to, because you're scared."

"Scared?" she demanded, her chin jutting out and her eyes darkening with anger to storm-cloud blue. "What am I supposed to be scared of? I've had real relationships. I'm not the one who—"

"Stop turning this on me," he interrupted her. "This is about *you*. This is about you being afraid to take a chance on what you want."

He knew she was going to argue, so he talked faster. "It's the same thing with your career as a negotiator. Do you understand why you still blame yourself for what happened? Do you?"

This wasn't the way he'd wanted to talk about the subject with her, but he was so angry, the words wouldn't stop. The more he tried, the faster and louder they came out. "It's not about whether or not you were ready to talk down Connors. It's not about your training or your skill."

"You don't know anything about that," Chelsie said, fury all over her face.

"It's about your mom's death," he continued ruthlessly. "It's about that man who died running to you, the man who had a one-year-old daughter at home. The man who'd never get to see his child grow up."

"Stop it!"

"Just like your mom never got to see you grow up."

"I said, stop it!"

"It's not your fault that man died! You're not

the one who kept him from seeing his daughter grow up," he said, practically yelling and mad at himself for doing it, but unable to stop. Why couldn't she see what she was denying herself? "You're a good negotiator. Don't give that up because you're scared!"

"It's not your business. Stop—"

"You and I have something good here, Chelsie, something real. Stop pushing me away because you're afraid of what will happen."

"Me?" Her voice was hard and angry, but her face had gone blotchy red, like she was trying not to cry.

"Yes, *you*. I want to be with you, Chelsie. I want—"

"You know what, Scott? Maybe I *am* scared, okay? Maybe you're right." Now, she was yelling, too. "But I'm not the only one, am I? You want to psychoanalyze me, Mr. Sniper? You think I'm a good negotiator? You think I can get into people's minds? Well, fine. Let me get into yours."

She jabbed her finger at his chest, so hard he took a step back. "You want to hear why I think you can't have a real relationship? You want me to tell you why everyone knows you're only good for one date before you move on? It's because *you're* scared."

"Oh, yeah? What am I scared of, Negotiator?"

"You're terrified that if you actually do allow yourself to care about someone long enough to date her, something will happen to her, just like it did to Maggie!"

As soon as the words were out, Chelsie clapped her hands over her mouth and her eyes went wide.

Scott staggered like she'd hit him. He shook his head, and opened his mouth to deny it, but what came out was a furious, "Well, it's too late for me not to care, Chelsie, because I love you!"

As far as least romantic declarations of love she'd ever received, Scott's won, hands down.

As soon as he blurted out that he loved her, he

went abnormally pale, then closed his eyes and let out a stream of really creative swear words.

Chelsie stared back at him, rooted in place. She didn't think she could speak if she wanted to, but she suspected Scott didn't want her to say anything. She had a feeling he not only hadn't meant to say the words, but that he didn't even realize he'd felt them.

Assuming he did mean them.

She felt herself go a little pale, too. Could he be serious? She studied him—head bent, fists clenched, shaking his head—and her chest got tight.

Did she want him to love her? The very idea panicked her, but underneath the fear, her heart was thumping an excited beat.

He lifted his head, his deep brown eyes pensive. "Sorry. I didn't—"

What? He didn't mean to say it? Didn't mean it?

When he stayed silent, she found her voice, although it came out strained. "Didn't what?"

"I didn't mean to yell at you."

Chelsie kept her eyes locked on him. Was there more? She waited, and the moment stretched until she had to speak. "It's okay," she said slowly, silently willing him to tell her whether or not he'd meant it.

A self-deprecating smile lifted his lips. "Anything you want to say?"

What did he want her to say? That she loved him back? That it was okay and she knew he didn't actually mean it?

"I..." The words stuck in her throat. How *did* she feel about Scott? She cared about him more than she wanted to, that was for sure. She hadn't been able to stop thinking of him in the past year, and in the past week and a half, he'd wormed his way into her thoughts so much she knew he'd never leave. He infuriated her and challenged her and excited her and the idea of letting him close enough that she could get hurt frightened her. But love?

"I don't know." How did she believe what she

was feeling if she wasn't even sure she could trust her own judgment?

She didn't realize she'd spoken the words out loud until he nodded solemnly, then said quietly, "Well, think about it. Figure out what you want to do. I want to date you, Chelsie. I want to give this thing between us a real chance. Not a fling, not a secret. So, you decide what you want and let me know."

"Okay," she managed, which seemed like a pitiful response.

He nodded, then actually kissed her hand, before leaving the room.

Once he was gone, she stayed in the center of the guest room in nothing but her underwear, not moving, for a long, long time.

Scott Delacorte wanted a serious relationship with her. He might even love her.

The question was, what the heck did she want? And did she have the courage to go after it?

HE WAS AN IDIOT.

The first woman he could actually imagine

creating a life with and he'd screamed at her about her shortcomings. And then he'd yelled at her that he was in love with her.

Way to be smooth, Scott chastised himself. If his behavior today didn't convince Chelsie he wasn't some accomplished ladies' man anymore, nothing would.

He actually felt sick to his stomach as he sat in his living room, staring blankly at the wall. He couldn't believe he'd said it at all. He hadn't realized he'd *felt* it, but now that it was out there— like a giant roadblock that stood in the way of getting Chelsie to give him a real chance—he knew it was true.

Being in love was supposed to make people happy, but all he felt was a little nauseated. Because the words he'd so tactlessly yelled at her might have been accurate, but she was right, too.

He'd never really thought about it, but the last time he'd been in a long-term, committed relationship with anyone had been right out of college. It had all fallen apart when Maggie was attacked. He'd blamed his ex-girlfriend for not giving him the space he needed to help his family, but hindsight told him she'd tried to be there for him, and he'd pushed and pushed until she'd given up on him.

Yeah, Chelsie was right. The idea of letting another person close and then having something happen to her, having that horrible, guilt-ridden feeling at not being able to stop it eat at him again, had made being alone sound pretty good. Until Chelsie, he'd never met anyone who made him think the chance might be worth it.

Figures he'd pick someone who didn't know how she felt. Figures that same woman would be in danger, too.

Because he couldn't protect her every hour of every day. Eventually, she'd have to go back to work. Eventually, she'd have to go back home. And once they nailed Hart to the wall, which he was determined to do fast, there were always threats. Especially with a job like hers.

Especially if she second-guessed every decision she made.

But even if she didn't feel the same way, even if she refused to go out with him, it wasn't going to change how he felt. It wasn't going to change that he was going to have to figure out a way to handle the thought of her in danger. Like he did with Maggie and Ella and Nikki and every other woman in his life.

Letting her get close might keep him up at night worrying more, but the rewards were greater, too. And hopefully the seasick feeling he had right now would eventually let up.

Scott leaned his head back against the chair, and looked at his watch. Chelsie hadn't left his guest room in over an hour. He almost got up to make sure she hadn't sneaked out the window, except this time, he had his car keys in his pocket.

What was he going to do if she finally emerged and told him she wasn't interested? He saw it on her face, even when he was screaming at her, that her feelings went beyond lust. The question was, how far beyond?

The door clicked open and he sat up straighter, clutching the arms of his chair as she came out of the room slowly, still in nothing but her bra and panties. She appeared serious, nervous, upset.

He had no idea if that was good or bad.

"Scott," she said, her voice so soft he had to lean forward to hear her.

Then she paused and, in the silence, he wanted to backtrack, tell her he didn't mean what he'd said about needing a real relationship. That he'd take whatever she was willing to give him, fling included.

But he kept his mouth shut. That wasn't good enough anymore. Not with her.

"Scott," she tried again. "I—"

The ringing of his phone cut her off. He hit *silent*, not glancing at the screen, but she said, "What if it's about the case?"

He frowned and glanced at his phone, immediately wishing he hadn't. It *was* the case agent, with horrible timing.

Swearing, he answered, putting Owen Jennings on speaker. "Delacorte."

"Uh, hi," Owen said, probably taken aback by his terse greeting. "I'm calling because we got the autopsy results on Connors."

"That was fast," Chelsie said, but she seemed a little relieved at the interruption.

"Yeah, well, technically Connors is still in autopsy, but I stepped out to call you, because we got the official determination."

"It wasn't suicide, was it?" Scott asked.

"No," Owen replied. "The medical examiner has ruled Connors's death a homicide."

Chapter Sixteen

"What've you got?" Scott asked Owen, still staring at Chelsie, willing her to look at him.

But her eyes were glued to the phone in his hands.

Not a good sign, but he'd deal with that later. Right now, he needed to focus on the case, on eliminating any remaining threat to Chelsie. If she planned to refuse him, he was going to make sure she was safe before she walked out that door.

The idea of her leaving made him feel even worse than the fact that he'd somehow managed to fall in love with her. He must have made some kind of noise, because she suddenly looked up at him questioningly.

Scott shook his head and turned his attention back to the phone call. *Focus*, he reminded himself.

"Well, the murder was different from Danvers's, which was pretty obviously a homicide. After that kill, whoever took out Connors tried to disguise it as a suicide. We've got gunshot residue on his hands and everything."

"So, what points to homicide?" Chelsie asked, the grim expression on her face an odd contrast to her sexy lingerie set.

"The weapon in Connors's hand was fired three times," Owen answered. "First on Danvers, then a bullet into Connors, then a final one into the ground."

"How do you know the order?" Scott asked, impatient.

"ERT did a good job of bagging Connors's hands at the scene. When we studied the GSR pattern, we discovered a pretty distinct area on

Connors's hand where there was no gunshot residue."

"Another pair of hands?" Chelsie guessed.

"You got it," Owen agreed. "Someone shot Connors in the head, at an angle that was plausible for suicide, then put the weapon in Connors's hands and fired it again to get GSR on him. He didn't expect us to be so thorough, I guess."

"That's someone with skill, to take out both Danvers and Connors up close like that," Scott said.

"Well, he was obviously armed," Owen replied. "Military or not, most people put their hands up and try to reason with whoever is holding the gun."

"But Danvers was in hiding—either from Connors or whoever took him and Connors out—and Connors was paranoid," Scott said. "I think both of them would've been walking around armed, too."

"Danvers had a weapon nearby," Owen confirmed. "Guess the killer sneaked up on him before he could go for it."

"What about Connors?" Chelsie asked.

"Only weapon we found was the gun he had in his hands. Which we assume was planted, since it killed Danvers. Of course, I suppose it's possible that Connors killed Danvers, then someone forced him to hand the gun over and shot him with it."

"Are we sure about the order?" Scott asked. "It wasn't Connors who was killed first?"

"We think Danvers was first, but it's possible."

Chelsie looked as if she was going to comment, but Owen said, "I gotta go back into autopsy. But I wanted to give you a heads-up."

"Is the Bureau putting Chelsie back into protective custody?" Scott asked.

"What for?" Owen replied. "It was Connors who was fixated on her. She owes this guy a thank-you for eliminating the threat."

"I don't think—" Chelsie started, but Owen cut her off.

"I'll call you back once I have more."

The call ended and Scott tucked his phone back in his pocket.

"I don't like it," Chelsie said.

"Me, either," Scott agreed. "You're staying here."

"That's…okay. That's not what I was talking about. I mean, I agree with you about this guy sneaking up on Danvers and Connors. How did he do that? Do you think they knew him?"

"If it was Hart, then Danvers would," Scott said. "It's possible he didn't view Hart as a threat. I am surprised Hart didn't take Connors out first, though."

"Because he seems like the bigger threat?"

"Yeah. And because he could have gotten Danvers to help kill Connors, then eliminated Danvers afterward. Plus, he could have used Connors's own gun on Danvers if he'd gone after Connors first, assuming he ordered Connors to hand it over." Scott thought about that a minute, then shook his head. A true marksman would never hand over his weapon. "Scratch that. He must have used a silencer on Danvers, then sneaked up on Connors—could've been while he was sleeping. By the time Connors realized he was there, it was too late. He shot Connors, then put the gun in his hands and took Connors's weapon—the one he had at the community center last week."

"So the gun in Connors's hands might have a trail," Chelsie said.

Scott nodded. "We should follow up on that. I doubt Hart is stupid enough to leave paperwork tying the gun to him, but who knows? I've definitely seen stupider."

Chelsie grinned. "Me, too."

With her smiling at him like that, he couldn't help himself. His gaze wandered down her nearly naked body, slowly, lingering. By the time he looked back into her eyes, she was bright red.

"I...uh, I should get dressed," she stammered, then rushed out of the room.

Instead of letting her go, he followed behind her, grabbing the door to his bedroom when she tried to shut it behind her.

She turned, apparently surprised to see him there. She crossed her arms over herself, like she was suddenly embarrassed. "What?"

"I want to know what you were going to say before."

"I'd rather have that conversation dressed."

Scott deflated. That didn't sound good. "You came out in your underwear," he reminded her.

"Yeah, well, I wasn't thinking."

He stepped closer. "Give it to me straight, Chelsie. Say what you need to say and I'll let you get dressed and we can focus on getting Hart into custody."

And once the threat was eliminated, he'd figure out how to convince her to give him a chance.

"Okay." She dropped her hands to her sides

and there were nerves in her voice when she asked, "Then tell me, were you serious?"

"Yeah, I was serious."

"About all of it? About—"

"Being in love with you? Yeah, I was serious."

"But…" She shook her head and he expected her to mention his track record with dating or how little time they'd really spent together, but what came out of her mouth was a bewildered "why?"

IF SCOTT DELACORTE was truly in love with her—and wasn't *that* something to wrap her brain around?—the real question was why?

Asking him probably made her sound needy or pathetic or both, but the reality was she hadn't been at her best lately. If Chelsie was being honest with herself, she hadn't been her best for a year.

Scott was right. She'd let the massacre destroy her career. Not in the FBI, but in the specialty where she belonged. Negotiation had made her happy. She'd known it was the right place for her the second she'd started training. And she'd let herself be driven away by her own fear.

And, although it hurt to think about it, he was probably right about her mom, too. Just the thought of that man running to her last year, crying about his one-year-old daughter, made her instinctively reach for her locket. It made her think of how she'd never gotten to know her mom, and how the man who'd begged for her help had a daughter who wouldn't remember him, either. She didn't need the crash course in psychology she'd gotten in negotiator training to recognize what she was doing. The only question was why she hadn't seen it before now.

It didn't change the fact that she hadn't made a difference that day. But maybe it meant she'd been holding on to it too long. Maybe it was time to start forgiving herself.

Perhaps it was time to let herself have the things she wanted. Scott included.

Scott's hand closed around hers, strong and

warm, and she realized she was still holding her locket. She saw understanding there in his eyes as he stepped closer to her. Her breath caught. Because she also saw another emotion that did look an awful lot like love.

"Why?" she asked again.

"You kept insisting this past week that I don't know you. But I do know you, Chelsie. You're smart and strong and despite what you believe, you're good at what you do."

He moved a little closer, not close enough to touch, except for their hands still linked over her locket, and let her see in his expression that he believed what he was saying. "You make me want more in my life."

A smile quivered on her lips and nervously, she joked, "Well, you did have me move in awfully fast."

Panic crossed his face, and before he blinked it away, she saw clearly how much Scott was putting out there. He'd called her on her faults and she'd denied them. She'd called him on his and here he was, trying to move past them. With her.

The idea that she would inspire that kind of change in Scott made her feel powerful. As if she could move forward, too. Perhaps she could even do it with him.

She was afraid he'd revert to what he'd always done. But she'd never find out if she didn't give him a chance to prove himself.

He believed in her, when she hadn't been able to believe in herself. Maybe she owed him the same.

"Is that what you were going to say when you came into my living room before?" Scott asked when she stayed silent too long. "You just wanted me to explain why?"

She smiled at him, feeling less burdened than she had in a long time. "Yes." She dropped her locket, but turned her hand over so she could lock her fingers through his. "Let's figure this case out, wait until things go back to normal and I'm home again. And then let's see what happens."

He squinted at her, a smile spreading on his face. "Is that your way of saying you'll date me?"

She felt herself smile with him. "Yes."

"Really dating? Not a fling?"

"Yes."

"Out in the open? Not a secret?"

Pushing back memories of what had happened in her old field office, Chelsie nodded. "Yes."

Scott's expression turned intense, and he dropped her hand. "Okay." He gestured to her clothes strewn on his floor. "Then hurry up and put some clothes on. We've got work to do. Let's get Hart behind bars. Because I'm ready for that date."

"THE GUN SEEMS like a dead end," Chelsie said, leaning back in her chair and rubbing her temples.

She'd been back to work for a day, but instead of returning to her regular white-collar crime squad, she was on loan to the case agents working the Connors and Danvers murders. Normally, the task would fall to the local cops, but because of the connection to the mass shooting, the FBI had gotten jurisdiction.

And the case agents had wanted her input, since, as they put it, Connors had bonded with her.

Scott had returned to work, too. She was still staying in the guest room at his house and he'd insisted on following her into work and following her home afterward. They'd agreed to put their personal relationship on hold until the case had been resolved.

At first, she'd been relieved. It would give her time to figure out exactly how she felt. But the more time she spent in Scott's house, the more she wanted to jump in and forget the consequences. And now that she was back at work, she missed him. Crazy as that was, since she'd seen him six hours ago.

"No trail?" Owen Jennings, the lead case agent, asked.

Chelsie shook her head, feeling way too confined in the small conference room, although it was bigger than the cubicle where she normally worked. "Those serial numbers were filed down pretty well. The lab only recovered a partial and some of it's guesswork, so not enough to be useful. I'm still running numbers, but without more, it's going to take a while. But none of the suspects have one registered with this partial. And the gun hasn't been connected to any other shootings. It's a virgin."

Every gun left behind a distinct pattern on the bullets it fired and the Bureau kept a database of those patterns. Which meant that often, when they ran a weapon from a crime scene, they could see that gun's entire sordid history— every time it had been fired in the commission of any other crime. But this one didn't have a history, as far as they knew.

"What about Connors?" Owen asked.

"He had several weapons registered to him, back before he went to prison. But he never owned any Berettas." Which was the weapon that had killed him.

"Well, your friend Hart seems to have a fondness for Berettas," Own said, laying a document in front of her.

The case had very quickly narrowed in on Hart once they'd found a payment in Danvers's account from right before the massacre. Scott had been right about Danvers not hiding his tracks particularly well and it had been easy to trace the payment back to Hart. Yet, when case agents had talked to everyone at the McCord camp, claiming a routine check because of Connors's ramblings at the community center, everyone there, including Hart, had denied knowing Connors or Danvers.

Proving that the money from Hart was a payoff for the massacre would take more, but combined with the phone calls she and Scott had found and Hart's denial of knowing Danvers when he clearly did, a federal judge had liked it enough to give them a little leeway. A warrant for Hart's records had come in about an hour ago.

They'd dug a little further into McCord and Rubenstein, too, but so far, nothing had popped with either of them. Both had alibis for the day Connors had caught her at the community center, which was the most likely place for someone to have picked up both Danvers's and Connors's trails.

"What do you think?" Owen asked, and Chelsie looked down at the document he'd handed her, which listed the weapons registered to Hart. Including three Berettas. None were the actual murder weapon, but that would be plain stupid.

"Weird," she said. "Why wouldn't he pick the type of weapon Connors used?"

"He might not have known," Owen said, taking the document back. "Or he might just have wanted a gun he was comfortable with when he faced Connors. He probably figured we'd never get this far, that Danvers and Connors would be ruled a murder-suicide, end of story."

Chelsie nodded, tucking her hair behind her ears. "Makes sense." But somehow she didn't like it. "Still…"

"It's enough," Owen said.

"What is?"

"Between the payment we found and the Beretta registrations and the final nail in his coffin." Owen grinned, looking proud of himself.

Chelsie frowned back at him. She'd never worked with Owen before, and she liked him fine, but he had a tendency to keep things close to his chest. He did take the time to verify his facts, but he was clearly fond of being the first to share. And he really liked the dramatic reveal. "Which is?"

"We got a call from forensics. We don't need that gun trail."

Chelsie tried not to roll her eyes for the hundredth time that day, wishing she was still running down leads with Scott. Even though they'd had fewer resources to do it, she preferred his company to Owen's. Or maybe it was just that she missed him; whether they were investigating a case, awkwardly digging for information about each other's personal lives, having an all-out argument or ripping each other's clothes off, she couldn't get enough of Scott.

She held in a smile, but Owen frowned at her. "What's funny?"

"Nothing," Chelsie said. "Spill it, Owen."

"Hart left a print."

"He did? Seriously?" He'd clearly been wearing gloves when he'd pressed the gun into Connors's hand and fired it to make sure gunshot residue was left behind. Why had he taken them off? "Where was it?"

"Remember the lighter we found next to Danvers's body?"

"Yeah." Beside the ratty old couch where

Danvers had died, a shiny, expensive lighter had rested on the side table. It had *Semper Fi* engraved on it, which made sense since Connors had been a Marine, though it was a little odd, since by all accounts, he'd never been a smoker.

"Liam Hart was a Marine, too," Chelsie realized.

"Yep. And he left a nice, clean print on it."

"Huh." The cabin had no electricity, so he'd probably taken the lighter out at one point for some light, then set it down and forgotten it. It wouldn't matter that he'd worn gloves if he'd handled it previously without them and had managed not to smudge those old prints. "Nice. So, we have a warrant for Hart's arrest?"

Was it really that simple? Excitement filled Chelsie, along with new nerves. If they could arrest Hart, it would be over. She and Scott could give this relationship a try.

"Not yet," Owen said, and Chelsie forced herself to focus. "But we're working on it right now. And we're taking your boyfriend with us."

"What?" Chelsie frowned. Rumors had already gotten out at work about her and Scott?

She pushed down her anxiety. This wasn't some forbidden affair between a supervisor and an employee like the false rumors in LA. She and Scott weren't on the same team, and if people started talking, at least there was no way they could say she'd been sleeping her way up the ladder.

Besides, she'd already agreed to his terms: a real relationship, no secret fling. And the reality was that it scared her, but she wanted him too much not to give him a real chance.

"Hart murdered an accomplished sharpshooter and another military guy who was expecting trouble," Owen said, obviously misunderstanding her question. "We're not messing around on this arrest. We're requesting snipers come with us. And I'm betting when we put that request in to HRT, your boyfriend is going to be the first to volunteer."

SCOTT RAISED HIS hand in the air, like he was back in school. "I'll go!"

Beside him, Andre gave a long-suffering sigh—mostly for his benefit, Scott was sure—and raised his hand, too.

At the front of the briefing room, Froggy rolled his eyes at them. "Figured you'd volunteer. The case agents were hoping for you two, anyway."

Froggy dismissed the rest of the team, who filed out of the room exchanging details about their evening plans.

It was Friday, Scott realized. The days had run together in the safe house, and he wasn't quite back in the swing of things yet.

"Hang on one sec, boss." He raced after the rest of the team, snagging Bobby's arm. "Bobby, can you do me a favor?"

The biggest guy on the team nodded seriously. "Let me guess. Pick up your girl?"

"Uh…" How had news gotten out so fast about him and Chelsie? "Well, she's got her Bureau vehicle, and we're about to arrest the guy I'm worried about. But can you follow her back from the WFO? She knows what's going down with this case, but I don't want her going home until Hart is behind bars. Follow her to my house, and check everything out before you leave, okay? Make sure she knows not to go anywhere until I get back?"

"Not a problem," Bobby said, holding out his hand.

Scott handed over his house keys and Chelsie's phone number. Hart shouldn't be able to slip past the cops who had eyes on his office, but Scott didn't want to take any chances. And although Chelsie was armed, Bobby was HRT, which meant regular training in close quarters combat and shooting skills. Not to mention that he was a tank of a guy who'd die before letting anyone get past him to a teammate's wife or girlfriend. "Thanks. I owe you one."

"Oh, don't worry," Bobby said, as he walked away, already dialing Chelsie to explain the change in plans. "I'll collect."

Scott held in a joke about lending out his bathtub after the next group outing at Shields, and went back into the conference room. The cops sitting on Hart at his office were supposed to call if Hart moved unexpectedly, but with Bobby watching over Chelsie, Scott could put his attention where it needed to be: on the mission.

"Sorry, boss," he told Froggy. "What are the specifics?"

"It's going to be pretty straightforward," Froggy said, addressing him and Andre. "The case agents would normally have enlisted SWAT on this one, except that Hart killed an accomplished sharpshooter. So they want you two set up before they go in, to be sure Hart doesn't come out shooting, or try to take a hostage."

"Why aren't they waiting until Hart goes home?" Andre asked. "No hostages there."

"Hart has a trip booked." Scott raised his eyebrows, but Froggy said, "He's had it booked for a month, but he's going straight to the airport from the office. So, this is good timing on the case agents' part. If they'd taken longer to line up the warrant, we'd have been in a mess."

"Easier to handle it here, in-house," Andre agreed.

"Especially since his trip is to the Caribbean," Froggy said. He laid out a drawing of the area around the McCord office. "It's in a federal building, so we're going to wait for him to go into the parking garage across the street before the case agents make the arrest."

Froggy tapped a building across from the garage. "You two will set up here. It should give you a good vantage point of most of the garage, including Hart's vehicle, which is where the case agents are set up. If it goes sour, you take him. Got it?"

That was simple. "No problem," Scott said, and Andre nodded.

"Then let's go," Froggy said. "The timetable is tight. We'll go over all the details on the drive."

"About time we wrapped this up," Andre said, slinging his rifle case over his back and striding to the door.

Silently Scott agreed. He wanted Chelsie completely, unquestionably out of danger from this case. He just hoped that once everything returned to normal—once she was back in her white-collar squad cubicle and her apartment and her regular life—that Chelsie wouldn't also return to her old refusal to date him.

Chapter Seventeen

The wind whipped around Scott as he lay flat on the roof of the courthouse, his eye lined up with the scope on his custom-built rifle. Heat from the sunbaked concrete beneath him seeped through his cargo pants and T-shirt. The scent of rain was in the air, mingling with the smell of steel and sweat.

Beside him, Andre also lay flat, but today he was the spotter. Scott was on the rifle. Which meant that if Hart made a move on the case agents waiting near his vehicle to arrest him, Scott had the authority to eliminate the threat.

A bullet through the head from Scott's rifle

meant instant death. No dying twitch that would allow Hart to get off a shot himself, if he drew on the case agents. If Scott had to do it, it wouldn't be the first time. But it was never the preferred solution.

Today, in particular, Scott wanted to hear what Hart had to say. Not that it really made a difference, but with Danvers and Connors dead, he wanted to hear Hart's explanation, guarantee no one else was involved before he considered it closed.

But where was Hart? They'd expected him an hour ago, but the only people Scott saw as he swept the parking garage were the case agents, squatted behind a Bureau van. Through his scope, they looked uncomfortable and antsy.

Hart's Mercedes was in his regular spot, and the cops who'd been watching the building hadn't reported him leaving. But everyone else from his office had already left. So, what was Hart doing? Was he still inside or had he managed to slip past the cops?

"Anything?" Scott asked Andre.

"Nope." Andre pressed the button on his radio. "Sierra One to TOC. Anyone have a lock on Hart?"

"Quit the sniper talk," Owen Jennings hissed. "We don't have him."

"What about inside?" Andre asked.

There was a long pause, then one of the other case agents came on. "I just passed his office. He's on his way out now. Stay sharp."

Finally. Scott rolled his shoulders and shook out his legs, getting more comfortable on the scope. His finger was outside the trigger guard, where it would stay unless he was planning to fire his gun.

"Got him," Andre said, and gave Scott the coordinates.

Scott adjusted his rifle and there was Liam Hart, exiting the elevator into the parking garage. He was alone, thank goodness, as Scott lined his head up neatly in the crosshairs of his rifle.

"No innocents in the vicinity," Andre reported.

Good. That meant Scott only had to worry about the case agents, who should be able to handle themselves.

"I've got control," Scott said into his radio, then clarified for the case agents who weren't used to HRT speak, "I have Hart in my scope. Stay in line with your current location and you won't block my shot."

Although the fact was, even if they moved, he'd still be able to take out Hart over their heads. He'd just prefer not to have to shoot that close to another federal agent unless necessary.

"Got it," Owen said quietly.

Through his scope, Scott watched Hart stroll toward his Mercedes, his hand digging in his pocket and coming out with a set of keys. He seemed completely oblivious to anyone else in the parking garage—apparently he really thought he'd gotten away with murder.

"Think again," Scott muttered, checking his

calibrations one last time to be sure they were adjusted properly for the wind and angle.

"Move now," Andre said into the radio, calm and efficient as always.

On cue, the case agents popped up from behind their van, weapons drawn. "FBI!" Owen yelled, his voice echoing off the concrete and making Scott's ears ring through the radio.

Hart jumped, his gaze darting around like he was contemplating making a run for it.

Scott kept his breathing even, his finger ready to slip inside the trigger guard if Hart made any move for a weapon.

"Liam Hart, cross your hands behind your head and get down on your knees," Owen ordered. "Slowly. Do it now!"

"You're under arrest," his partner, Pete Shore, added.

"For what?" Hart demanded, and through his scope, Scott could see the pulse beating frantically at his neck.

Through his scope, Scott could see the way

his eyes darted back and forth, the way his hand clenched his keys until his knuckles turned white. Through his scope, Scott could see his guilt.

It was there in his desperate expression. Hart looked panicked. But he wasn't bewildered. He knew why the agents were there.

"Get down on your knees," Owen insisted again, taking a step closer, his weapon drawn and his grip tense.

"Go easy," Scott murmured.

Hart glanced back and forth between the agents again, then his head turned toward the door. But instead of running, he sank to his knees, his hands still lingering near his pockets.

One of them twitched, like he was considering reaching inside, where he might have a weapon.

Scott kept his rifle steady, his breathing slow, and his heart rate down, in case he needed to fire.

Hart's hand twitched toward his pocket once

more, then resignation crossed his face and he put his hands over his head.

As Owen rushed over and cuffed him, Pete said, "You're under arrest for the murder of Mike Danvers and Clayton Connors."

"THE MEDIA IS reporting that Connors killed himself after he shot this Danvers guy," Hart said. He sat in an interview room at the FBI office, arms crossed tightly over his chest, his expression tense and guarded.

"You tried to make it look that way, didn't you?" Owen demanded, as Scott and Andre watched through the one-way glass on the other side of the room.

Hart's lawyer, a reed-thin man with sharp eyes, leaned close and whispered in his ear.

Hart waved him off, his lips curling. "Of course not. I had nothing to do with it. We are talking about Clayton Connors, right? The guy who murdered a bunch of people last year?"

"You should know *that*, too," Pete said, still

standing, despite the empty seat next to his partner. "Since you milked it for all it was worth to get McCord's bill passed."

"The McCord-Siler bill," Hart corrected him. "And yeah, of course I know. Who doesn't? That doesn't mean I had anything to do with his death."

Scott rubbed his eyes and slumped against the wall. They'd been at it for over an hour now, most of the time spent waiting for Hart's attorney to arrive. Once the adrenaline rush of being on the rifle had worn off, Scott was ready to crash.

"I can call you if Hart confesses," Andre offered for the third time.

He was annoyingly alert, probably because of the WFO coffee he'd been drinking by the gallon. The WFO agents seemed to have as much expertise in making coffee as Andre did.

"I'm not leaving until we're sure." Scott told his partner the same thing he'd said the last two times he'd asked.

"Even if McCord knew—"

"I know. Hart is the physical threat. But I want this closed. I want to be able to go home and tell Chelsie with complete certainty that it's over."

"She's waiting for you at home, huh?" Andre asked, amusement in his tone.

Scott refused to get riled up. "You know I wasn't ready to call off the protective detail."

Andre grinned. "Oh, is that what you're calling it?"

"Don't be a smart-a—"

"Yeah, yeah." Andre seemed ready to say more, but stopped when Hart's lawyer spoke up.

"Your evidence against my client is slim. This is about some lighter? Liam here hasn't seen that lighter in a week. Someone could have taken it."

"And managed not to smudge Hart's fingerprint?" Owen sounded skeptical.

"Sure seems like your client had a reason to

want Connors and Danvers quiet," Pete said conversationally.

"I didn't know—" Hart started, but his lawyer raised a hand and cut him off.

"No?" Owen jumped on it anyway. "That's what you told the case agents at McCord's office, too, but there's a pretty big payment to Mike Danvers from your personal account last year."

"I—" Hart started.

His lawyer cut him off. "My client will have to check his financial records to verify what this alleged payment was for."

"Oh, cut it out!" Owen snapped. "You claim you didn't know Danvers, and yet right before the massacre that Connors says Danvers talked him into, there's a payment from you to Danvers for twenty grand. And conveniently, your lighter shows up next to Danvers's body."

"It could've been planted," his lawyer said, but Scott leaned closer to the glass because Hart was starting to squirm.

"I had nothing to do with that!" Hart burst out.

His lawyer put a hand on his arm and leaned close again, but Hart shook him off. "I did *not* go anywhere near Mike Danvers or Clayton Connors. How would I even have known where they were? I didn't touch them!"

"Liam," his lawyer tried again, but Hart gave him a nasty look that shut him up.

"Okay, I paid Mike. But it's not…it was for a…a personal loan. When the FBI agents came asking about him and Connors in the same breath, I knew Mike had to be connected to Connors, and I didn't want to get sucked into that. So I said I didn't know Mike. But I didn't kill him!"

Scott glanced at his partner. Andre had set down his coffee and was frowning.

Hart was definitely lying. But was he lying about all of it? Beneath the desperation was something else, something that seemed a lot like anger.

Anger that he'd been caught? Possibly. But he'd been really mad when they brought up the lighter. Was it because he was mad at himself for leaving it behind? Or could there be truth to his claim that someone was setting him up?

Unwilling to sit on the sidelines any longer, Scott turned away from the glass and left the room.

"Hey!" Andre said, running after him.

Scott picked up his pace, so his partner couldn't stop him, then opened the door to the interview room.

Everyone looked over at him. Hart and his lawyer with surprise, Owen and Pete with annoyance.

"Who set you up?" Scott demanded. Hart was definitely involved. Which meant that if he didn't kill Connors and Danvers himself, he still knew who did.

"Don't answer that," Hart's lawyer barked, at the same time that Owen yelled, "Get out of here, Delacorte!"

Pete came toward him, probably to try to physically push him out the door, as Andre came up behind him and grabbed his shoulder.

But neither of them got him out of the room before Hart jumped to his feet and shouted, "Mark! It was Mark Rubenstein!"

CHELSIE TOOK HER head out of Scott's refrigerator and strained to listen. Was that her phone?

Hearing nothing, she shook her head and continued to consider her current food options. Deciding to eat Scott's leftover Chinese takeout from last night, she put it on the counter and glanced at her watch.

Scott had called an hour and a half ago to give her the news that Hart was under arrest. He was staying at the WFO until they had Hart's confession.

She'd considered joining him there, but decided to wait. But every minute that passed without Scott returning home cranked her nerves up a little more. Not because she was worried Hart wouldn't confess—it might take a while, but the evidence was there. He'd done it.

No, she was nervous because arresting Hart meant it was time to make good on her promise to have a real relationship with Scott.

Suddenly not hungry, Chelsie stuck the food back in the fridge. She hadn't really put herself out there, for anything, since Connors had massacred those nine people. She'd gone safe, with work, with relationships, with everything. And now, her first real test, her first big risk was with Scott. And she was afraid she was going to screw it up.

Letting out a breath, Chelsie sank onto the nearest chair. It wasn't Scott she was worried about at all, she realized. Not really. And it wasn't fear of how people would react at work. Those were concerns, sure. But Scott was right. The real problem was her.

Even now, even after she'd made the decision to give him a chance, she was still doubting her own judgment. Still scared she'd make a mistake and would lose big.

Frustration built up in her chest. Clayton Connors was dead, but he still had this power over her. Would she ever stop second-guessing herself?

She looked up at the picture on Scott's kitchen wall of his sisters and him as kids. Just like now, as a teenager, he oozed charm. But it wasn't superficial. She could see from the way he held his baby sister, from the way he and Maggie stood, that he was close to them. Everyone liked Scott. It was hard not to like him.

He was a good guy. He'd volunteered for her protection detail despite her rebuking him over and over. And when she would have jumped right back into bed with him, he'd actually put on the brakes to prove himself to her.

He loved her. And judging by the way terror flooded her at the thought of messing things up, she was pretty sure she loved him, too.

A nervous giggle escaped and Chelsie covered her mouth, glad Scott wasn't there to hear it.

She loved Scott Delacorte.

She let the idea roll around in her head, and recognized it was true. She wasn't sure when it had happened, but it was definitely love.

A smile started to form and Chelsie stood. Maybe she couldn't change her fear. But she could stop letting it rule her life. And she was going to start with Scott.

If he was determined to prove himself by going out on three dates with her before taking their physical relationship any further, then she could show him that she was committed to making it work, too. The case was almost solved, which meant they could have their first date when he got home tonight.

She opened the fridge again, cataloging the ingredients, and nodded to herself. Hopefully Hart wouldn't cooperate for another hour, and she'd have just enough time to cook a decent dinner, change into something a little sexier and show Scott she wasn't planning to back out.

Abandoning the food for now, Chelsie went to go through the bag of clothes from the safe house and pick out her best option. There weren't many choices, but from the way Scott had looked at her even when she had on day-old, rumpled cargos and a T-shirt, she could make it work.

Chelsie unclipped her gun and handcuffs, then set them on the side table and started digging through her bag. There really were slim pickings, but she took out the best of the bunch: snug-fitting jeans and a scoop-neck tank.

She was about to pull her T-shirt off when she heard the door from the garage click open. Scott was back.

Wishing she'd thought to do this an hour earlier, Chelsie went into the kitchen to meet him. They could go out to dinner instead. Celebrate the beginning of their relationship.

"How did the interrogation go?" she asked, smiling, as she rounded the corner.

But instead of finding Scott in the kitchen, Mark Rubenstein stood next to the counter, wearing all black and looking grim. "Hopefully, Hart is holding his tongue," he answered conversationally, as though she'd intended the question for him.

The expression on his face told her the conversation wasn't going to last long. He seemed intense, as if he was going into battle, and she remembered that before he'd started Blackgate, he'd been a special operations soldier.

Chelsie froze, panic sinking low in her gut. Could she make a run for the bedroom, where she'd left her gun?

Before she could move, Mark moved away from the counter, and she saw the Beretta clutched in his hand. His gloved hand.

The panic turned into dread as she looked

back up into his eyes, which were cold and unforgiving.

"Chelsie Russell," he snarled. "You're a hard
woman to get alone."

Chapter Eighteen

"She's not picking up the phone," Scott muttered, then added a string of curses and put the driver's training the FBI had given him to good use.

Instead of reminding him that he could hear the speaker phone, too, Andre just reached up and held on to the bar over his head as Scott sped around cars on I-95.

Horns blared all around him as he whipped left, went around a truck, then sped right to pass another car. He'd already stuck the siren on top of his vehicle, but rush-hour traffic hadn't totally cleared yet, so it wasn't helping a whole lot.

"What about Bobby?" Andre asked.

"He dropped her off almost an hour ago. He said everything was fine then."

"It probably still is," Andre said. "There's no reason for Rubenstein to know we have Hart in custody. And even if he did, chances are pretty slim that he'd be looking for Chelsie or that he'd be able to find her."

"He found Connors and Danvers," Scott said, most of his attention on the road as he drove along the divider, inches away from the concrete wall.

"He had an alibi for the night Connors caught up to Chelsie at the community center," Andre reminded him.

"Right. Which means that Hart is probably the one who was following Danvers, and he told Rubenstein."

"But if Rubenstein stayed on Danvers, he couldn't also follow Chelsie."

Scott knew Andre was trying to make him feel better, but the truth was, Chelsie wasn't in hiding anymore. And if Connors could track down Ella at home, Rubenstein, with his Spec Ops background, could probably find Chelsie at his house.

He pounded a hand against the wheel. "I shouldn't have left her alone. I should have made Bobby stay with her."

It was shades of Maggie all over again. Back then, he hadn't known someone was watching his sister until it was way too late. But the helplessness he'd felt that day had been with him ever since.

And today, if Rubenstein *did* find Chelsie, he'd probably kill her.

"There was no reason for us to think Hart had help until now. No reason for you to ask Bobby to stick around," Andre insisted. "And Chelsie is armed."

"Rubenstein was a SEAL." Rubenstein could slip into a house and snap someone's neck before they knew he was there, including an armed federal agent. Scott knew because he'd trained with a group of SEALs once.

Even with his own specialized training, he didn't want to go up against a former SEAL who'd gone bad. And Chelsie had spent the past year doubting every decision she made. If she had a shot at Rubenstein, would she take it? Or would she hesitate one second too long?

"He's probably not there," Andre was saying. "We're probably worrying for nothing."

But there was tension in his voice that betrayed exactly how worried he was.

"Just in case, though," Andre continued, "let's figure this out."

"I'll go in through the garage," Scott said, already running through the possible entry points in his mind. "You go through the basement window in the back and come up the stairs. The front and back doors don't have any concealment once you get in."

"If Chelsie's okay, we're going to scare the heck out of her," Andre said.

"Yeah, well, better scared than hurt," Scott muttered. His heart rate was way too fast, and it didn't matter how many techniques he'd learned as a sniper to slow it down. None of them were working.

Chelsie was in trouble. He could feel it. And he wasn't there to help her.

SHE WAS GOING TO DIE.

Chelsie backed up slowly, but there was nowhere to go. She couldn't make it out of the kitchen and down the hall faster than he could raise that gun and pull the trigger.

Rubenstein silently watched her, not seeming concerned. He might not realize she didn't have her holster on under her T-shirt, but he definitely knew he had the upper hand.

If she tried to run, he'd shoot. That was clear from his stony expression. And what good would talking do?

She kept moving backward, inch by inch,

until she hit the wall. The picture of Scott and his sisters rattled as she bumped it.

A lump formed in her throat as she realized Scott was going to come home from the WFO, thinking the case was solved, and find her dead. And it didn't matter that it wasn't his fault. Just like with what happened to Maggie, he'd never forgive himself for not somehow knowing. For not somehow stopping it.

Chelsie took a step forward.

Rubenstein's eyebrows lifted, but it was the only sign he was surprised. "If you're planning to rush me, I'd rethink that."

"No, I'm not."

"Good. Then let's be straight with each other. I'm going to kill you."

Fear clamped down and Chelsie fought it, resisted the primal urge to scream or run. Neither would do her any good.

Rubenstein moved over to lean against the counter. He continued conversationally, "But how you go is up to you. I'll make it fast if you cooperate. I just need a few answers. Be straight with me and this will go easy for you. Lie to me?" He pressed his lips together. "Well, then we'll find out exactly how much pain you can take before you give in."

"You know Hart is in custody," Chelsie said. She was surprised to hear her voice come out calm, in control, the way it had when she'd been in negotiator training.

"He won't talk," Rubenstein said, sounding certain. "He knows what will happen if he talks."

"Right now, he's the only one we're looking at for the murders of Connors and Danvers," Chelsie said. "You kill me while he's in custody, and you're going to invite a bigger investigation."

Rubenstein shrugged. "It can't be helped, but they'll never pin it on me. I need to figure out what kind of damage control I'm looking at now. So you're going to tell me and then I'll make this quick. You won't even feel it."

Chelsie tried to steady her nerves. Rubenstein

sounded way too blasé about the idea of murdering a federal agent. How was she going to convince him to let her live? He'd already admitted his guilt by coming here; he had to realize there was no turning back. Which meant he had to go through with it, unless she could show him that he'd only be making things worse.

Even if he'd paid Hart to ensure that the bill passed, they couldn't tie him to the massacre itself. And if Hart had killed Danvers and Connors, Rubenstein hadn't committed murder yet. Was that enough?

She had a bad feeling it wasn't, but she had to try. "You don't have blood on your hands yet, Mark. You can't really believe that murdering a federal agent and getting the Bureau to chase after my killer is going to make things better for you."

"You honestly think Liam Hart got his hands dirty? From a distance, he can do it—it was his idea to go to Danvers. Originally, he thought he could convince Danvers to be our example. But when he tried to lay the groundwork there, Danvers just kept ranting about Connors. About what a mess he was, high on pills to numb his pain when everyone else in his unit had died and he was really the lucky one. Blah blah blah."

Rubenstein rolled his eyes and Chelsie tried not to let her disgust show. The man had no empathy at all.

"So I checked Connors out myself. I went to one of the veterans' support groups. Sat in the back and listened to Connors talk and I knew we could use him. So, I told Hart to go through Danvers to reach Connors. It worked, too, and making Danvers the connection kept us at a distance. All Danvers wanted was a little money and the promise of a job. It would have all been fine if Connors hadn't run." He frowned. "And Connors ran to *you*. Why is that?"

Ignoring the question, Chelsie asked, "You

killed Danvers and Connors? And then you framed Hart?"

"Yeah," he said, as though he couldn't believe it had taken her so long to figure it out. "Framing Hart was a backup, of course. I thought the murder-suicide would fly. I asked Danvers about you while I was there, but he didn't know what Connors told you. And Connors? Well, I wanted his death to pass as a suicide, so I couldn't get persuasive. Besides, he hadn't gone soft like Danvers. I didn't want to mess around there. But that meant I couldn't be certain how much Connors had worked out. He couldn't know about me. But if he knew about Hart, if he'd given you Hart's name, then it seemed like a good idea to serve him up as my backup plan."

"So why come after me, then, if you had it all worked out?"

"Because this morning, my secretary realized she'd forgotten to tell me someone had called for me last week, but refused to give a name. And what did I find but that call had come from a federal line." He shook his head and raised his weapon, lining up with her face. A kill shot. "That was you, wasn't it?"

Actually it had been Scott, but Chelsie nodded, trying not to let him see her fear. "But I ruled you out. We arrested Hart. It was over."

She knew trying to convince him that she wouldn't say anything if he let her live was a losing battle. He'd never believe that from a federal agent. So, she ran through everything she knew about Rubenstein, searching her memory for a way to connect with him. Her instinct said that getting him to see her as a person wasn't going to work. This guy was a narcissist. Possibly even a sociopath, judging by the way he was talking about the men he'd set up and then murdered. He wouldn't care.

She had to focus on him, focus on why killing her wasn't in his best interest. But how? Panic bloomed. She didn't know.

She *was* going to die, right here in Scott's kitchen.

Regrets raced through her mind. Regret that she hadn't fought harder for the career she'd loved. Regret that she hadn't gone out with Scott when she had the chance.

Worst of all, she was going to die exactly the way she'd feared. Because when it came to the real thing, she wasn't a good enough negotiator.

Maybe it was fate. Connors had spared her a year ago, but perhaps it had always been a temporary reprieve.

At least this time, she wouldn't take anyone else with her.

Even as the thought entered her mind, a movement behind Rubenstein made her flinch. She covered up her reaction by blurting, "You could have gotten away with it. Killing me is digging your own grave!"

"Well, I've told you too much, so I don't have a choice now, do I?" Rubenstein asked, sounding a little too gleeful about it.

Behind him, in the crack of the garage doorway, Scott stood, one hand in the door frame next to his weapon. But she knew he didn't have the right angle.

Rubenstein was standing in front of the kitchen counter, and the cabinets above blocked his head. The best option Scott would have was to fire at Rubenstein's gut. But that wouldn't prevent Rubenstein from shooting as he fell, and the Beretta was aimed at her head. And that *was* a kill shot.

If Scott moved into the room, Rubenstein would see him and try to shoot. Scott was good, but Rubenstein had similar training. Chelsie wasn't sure who would win that match and she didn't want to find out. Especially since Scott would have to clear the doorway, putting him in the open while Rubenstein could duck below the counter. She suspected that even if Scott hit Rubenstein, he'd get hit in the process. And she couldn't allow that to happen.

"So, what we're going to do," Rubenstein continued, "is discuss exactly what Connors told you, and exactly what you documented, so I can decide on my damage control."

Chelsie clenched her fists, and from the way Rubenstein's eyes went to her hands, she could tell he was checking to see that she wasn't making a fast move for a weapon. He didn't know she was unarmed. Maybe she could use that to her advantage.

Connect, Chelsie reminded herself, calling on her negotiator training. Figure out what he wants, and find a way to give it to him. End this without bloodshed.

Behind Rubenstein, Scott started to move very, very slowly.

Fear burst forth so strong that Chelsie bit down on her tongue. "There's only one way to control the damage now," Chelsie said, speaking fast, and putting as much confidence as she could into her voice. Simultaneously, she shook her head the tiniest amount, praying Scott would understand what she wanted him to do, and would trust her.

In the doorway behind Rubenstein, Scott froze, but from her peripheral vision, she could see he was torn. He wanted to move. He wanted to rush in and, if he had to, he'd put himself in danger to save her.

"Okay, I'll bite," Rubenstein said, sounding amused.

But underneath the sarcasm, Chelsie heard genuine interest. The confidence she'd forced into her voice began to fill her. She had him. She could do this.

Trust your gut, she told herself.

"You only have one choice and I'm sure you know it," she went on, thinking about his narcissism. He'd have to pretend, or pretend he knew better. Either way, she could get him to see what he really needed.

He frowned at her, as though he suspected she was trying to play him.

"You have to run."

He laughed, but it sounded forced.

"What other option is there?" Chelsie went on.

"Either way you play this right now, you've left behind a mess. Kill me, and the FBI is never going to stop hunting for the person who did it."

"They—"

"I've been in hiding for the past week and a half. There's only one case I'm on, and it's yours. So, they'll assume Hart was working with someone."

Rubenstein's frown deepened.

Not wanting to give him too much time to think about the position he'd put himself in until she'd led him to the conclusion *she* wanted him to form, she said quickly, "Or you leave, and I tell them it's you. Either way, you're the only other person I suspected."

"You must have—"

"I called you, right? That's documented on our end, too, Mark. The FBI is going to come looking for you. And even if you don't leave behind a single piece of evidence here—which is forensically pretty unlikely, you know—the

FBI won't rest if you kill one of their own. You know that, of course."

He scoffed at her again, but it lacked the amusement he'd shown earlier. "So, you're saying I'm screwed either way?"

"I'm saying you need to run. And I'm suggesting that you do it without murdering a federal agent."

"And then what? You tell them it's me and the FBI still comes after me." He shook his head, but shifted his weight again as he did it, and Chelsie knew he was following her trail.

She *could* do this.

"If you run without hurting me, we might not be able to pin Connors and Danvers on you, and we only have so many resources to spend investigating the deaths of men who planned a massacre. But you kill me, and you honestly think the FBI will *ever* stop hunting you?"

Rubenstein swore at her. "You expect me to believe that your going on the stand and saying I confessed won't seal my fate?"

"Just my word and no physical evidence?" Chelsie asked. "It's really hard to say. But you kill me, and you're the only suspect. And my death is one the FBI will be absolutely positive they close."

Rubenstein's gun hand came down a little as he stared at her.

She could see it in his eyes. He was finally realizing the position he'd put himself in.

Which meant he was considering his options now. And there were only a few. Run, like she'd suggested, and he'd run smack into Scott. Try to kill her anyway. Or—possible, though un-likely—kill himself.

She needed to prepare for any option, so she stepped toward him, moving right as she did so, forcing Rubenstein to shift with her.

"What are you doing?" he asked as he moved slightly away from the cabinets.

Enough to give Scott a head shot? She didn't know.

"You have the skills to hide," she told him, as she saw Scott, slipping forward a little, in her peripheral vision. "Don't give the FBI a reason to plaster your name and face everywhere as the prime suspect in the murder of a federal agent."

Rubenstein's lips twisted, and she realized she'd pushed too far and hit a nerve. His name would be plastered on the news either way, and he had to know it.

"You have one opportunity to save yourself. Walk out that door now."

Rubenstein glanced down at his feet, and as his eyes came back up, she knew.

Nothing she was going to say would have changed the outcome. He'd come here to kill her, and that's what he was going to do.

He started to lift the gun back up, and Chelsie knew that now it was time to trust herself—she knew she was out of options—and trust Scott to have her back.

"Now!" she screamed, diving to the ground.

Two shots rang out, so close together she couldn't tell who'd fired first.

And then both men fell to the floor.

Epilogue

"It's official," Chelsie announced, a huge grin on her face and pride obvious in her voice.

That grin—too big for her face and way too infectious—was what had grabbed him from the very first day he'd met her. Scott couldn't help himself from smiling back. "You're in?"

"I'll have to shadow Martin Jennings on a few cases first, but, yes, I'm back."

She sure was. Scott let his gaze drift over her, from the top of her wheat-blond hair, over the heart locket and down the length of her figure-hiding pantsuit. By the time his eyes lifted back to hers, she was blushing.

But instead of backing away, she put her arm through his and whispered, "Two more dates."

He'd officially taken her on their very first date last night. If she'd have agreed, he would have made it a week ago, but after he'd been shot by Rubenstein, she'd insisted he stay in bed until the doctor cleared him to go back to work.

He'd tried to argue that the bullet in his leg was a flesh wound, that he'd had worse, but she refused to listen, probably because it had bled like crazy all over his kitchen. She had, however, stayed in his guest room to take care of him, so he couldn't complain too much. Not to mention that as soon as Andre had run into the room and kicked the gun away from Rubenstein, she'd rushed over and tried to stop the bleeding with her bare hands, ignoring all protocol. The whole time, she'd demanded that he be okay, because she loved him.

She loved him. That thought made his grin wider. He couldn't wait until their next date.

"Does today count?" he asked, stepping closer so his body brushed hers with every step.

She was still smiling at him, and he realized that once she'd accepted he was truly okay, she'd barely stopped smiling.

With Rubenstein dead and the case officially closed, he'd expected her to be wary and slow things down with him, but she'd done the opposite. Negotiating with Rubenstein long enough to let Scott maneuver into a position to take him out seemed to have restored the confidence she'd been missing for the past year. And with it, all her spunk and determination had come back, too. She'd even returned to negotiation.

He was proud of her, and anxious to take their relationship to the next level. But was she ready for *this*? Scott held open the door for her. "Ready?"

He held his breath as he waited for her answer. He'd been ready for a long time, ready to prove to her that she was no one-night stand to him, that he wanted more than a short, secret fling. The question was: did she finally believe it?

She seemed nervous as she straightened her jacket and nodded, stepping through the door.

At the back of the coffee shop, Maggie and Ella were waiting. He saw them look at his and Chelsie's locked arms and exchange a glance.

As they sat down, Scott noticed the dark circles under his sister's eyes, but she smiled at him, and he knew she didn't want him to worry about her today. He hoped it was just work, and not something new with the Fishhook Rapist, but now wasn't the time to ask. Like with Chelsie, he had to trust her. When she needed him, she'd ask for his help.

Ella's expression was eager and curious. "So, this is serious, huh?"

Scott laughed. He should have known Ella wouldn't be able to hold her tongue long enough for them to order coffee.

Before he could answer, Chelsie slipped her hand into his under the table. "It is serious."

Scott couldn't help himself. He pulled her to him and kissed her, hard and fast.

Across the table, Ella held out her hand to Maggie. "Pay up."

Scott tried to glare at them, but his smile ruined it. "You betting on me?"

Ella appeared proud of herself as she said, "I bet her that you and Chelsie would be serious by the time that protective detail was over."

"And you took the bet?" Scott teased his sister, feigning hurt. "You didn't think Chelsie would fall for my charms?"

Beside him, Chelsie's fingers stroked his wrist, and he knew he was the one who'd fallen for her charms.

Ella tapped the table. "Pay up!"

"Not so fast," Maggie said, and a smile lit up her face, making her seem more carefree than Scott had seen her in a while.

She leaned across the table, her gaze going back and forth between him and Chelsie. "Tell me, big brother. Who exactly have you been mooning over for the past year?"

He gaped at her, then glanced at Chelsie, who looked surprised, too. "You knew?"

Maggie leaned back in her seat. "Being SWAT doesn't make me all brawn and no brains," she joked. Then she held her own hand out and glanced at Ella, who mumbled under her breath and slapped some bills into it.

Beside him, Chelsie leaned closer, until their arms were pressed tightly together, and asked Maggie, "But did you know I was mooning over him, too?"

Scott smiled at her. "You were? For a year?"

As she gazed up at him and nodded, the rest of the coffee shop seemed to fade in to the background. Vaguely, he heard Maggie and Ella say something about getting them some coffee as they stood up.

But it was Chelsie's voice he heard clearly as she took a handful of his shirt and yanked him down to her. "I did fall for your charms," she whispered. Then, right before she pressed her lips to his, she added, "I love you, Scott Delacorte."

He was smiling as he kissed her back, not wanting to ever stop. He'd finally done it. He'd finally proven to Chelsie that for him, she'd always been a long-term plan.

Now it was time to show her that this was just the beginning. And he was more than ready.

* * * * *

MILLS & BOON®

Why shop at millsandboon.co.uk?

Each year, thousands of romance readers find their perfect read at millsandboon.co.uk. That's because we're passionate about bringing you the very best romantic fiction. Here are some of the advantages of shopping at www.millsandboon.co.uk:

✳ **Get new books first**—you'll be able to buy your favourite books one month before they hit the shops

✳ **Get exclusive discounts**—you'll also be able to buy our specially created monthly collections, with up to 50% off the RRP

✳ **Find your favourite authors**—latest news, interviews and new releases for all your favourite authors and series on our website, plus ideas for what to try next

✳ **Join in**—once you've bought your favourite books, don't forget to register with us to rate, review and join in the discussions

Visit **www.millsandboon.co.uk**
for all this and more today!